D1527106

for Ian

Thank you for challenging me.

Minotaur

One

Dear Diary,

I feel a little silly writing that, but I've always wanted to. Growing up, that's what I always saw in books and movies and TV. And it feels a little less lonely than just writing to myself every day. So dear diary, I have so many things to tell you. Should I start with myself? Okay.

My name is Silly. Isn't that funny? My mom named me Priscilla, but I was so cute and precious my dad shortened it to Silly when I was just a baby, and it's stuck with me ever since. There were plenty of times in my life that I wasn't a big fan, but now, in high school, it's something kinda cool that sets me apart just enough to be noticed, not enough to be that weird girl. Nobody wants to be that weird girl. I feel so bad for her sometimes. More about that later. I need to finish telling you about myself so that in a million years when some alien archaeologists discover this diary they know who I am!

I'm 15 years old, and I have a little brother who's 9. He's okay. We get along a lot better than most other kids and their little brothers or sisters. We play Monopoly together, and Scrabble and other games sometimes. He minds his own business and I mind mine. We have this understanding where we don't tell our mom on each other. Oh, and his name is Justin.

My mom manages the apartment complex where we live, that's why we live here instead of in a real house like we used to when I was little, and dad was still alive. It's kind of cool, kind of not, because I do have a harder time making friends with new renters once they find out who my mom is and how she can kick them out in the street anytime she wants. It's not really like that, though. My mom's fair, and wouldn't do that just because I said something bad about somebody. It's enough for me that I know that and my mom knows that, so it's not that big of a deal anyway.

Yeah, my dad died when I was five, before my brother was even born yet. A drunk driver hit him and walked away, and my dad died right there. It's hard to see some of the other girls with their dads sometimes, but then I think about the memories I do have of my dad, and I feel like at least I have those few good times with him. That's another reason I like my name being Silly, because my dad gave it to me. That's worth way more than even the whole school making fun of me. I do sometimes worry that because of what happened, I won't get invited to parties and stuff where there's drinking, but I'd rather get invited and not drink and make sure other kids get home safe than stay home and worry that another family will have to go through what we did.

Sometimes it seems kinda strange to me that something that happened when I was so young, that I didn't understand at the time other than my dad was gone, can affect my whole life so much. But I guess it's like history class, when you understand more about things that happened a long time ago, you can learn a lesson from it that you keep with you always. But it is one of those things that make adults look at me in that way, like I'm too young to be so mature. They don't really understand that it's your brain that makes you mature, not how long you've been alive. Sometimes you just know things that make sense, and you have to try to help other people understand them because everyone needs to know how much sense they make. Does that make sense?

Wow, I didn't realize I'd have so much to say before I really said much! I've had diaries before, but I would just write little notes here and there, like two or three times a year, and nothing really important. It feels different now, like what I'm saying is more important. I don't know why, I'm 15. I haven't achieved anything great with my life, and I'm sure I won't for years and years. But it's good to feel good, so I'll go with that. Plus it's fun to imagine that someone could be reading this in a million years to learn about humans today!

Okay, okay, what else about me? I like school. I'm not one of those kids who gripe about having to go, because I really do like it! It's easy, but I do learn new things, especially in math and science. What I really like is writing, though. I write stories for English class and then read them aloud, and everyone usually likes them. They're not very long, and mostly stuff like fairy tales, but it's something fun that doubles as homework, so it's a win-win. I'm not a big nerd though, I do have other hobbies and friends and stuff. I like to read and go shopping and try on clothes. I don't get to buy too many, but it's always fun to go try new stuff on and see how it looks. We have a pool, and I go swimming a lot. It'll be warm enough to start swimming again soon, so I'm pretty excited about that!

My best friend's name is Julia, and she even lives in our apartment complex, which is awesome.

My mom's calling me, so I'll write more later! Gotta earn my keep! Bye for now, diary!

Two

"Silly! I thought you wanted to make some money for some new clothes or something!!" called Rachel. She thought to herself what a blessing it was to have an honest, dependable teenager, not one of those reckless, crazy girls that are always in the news for something. *Silly really is a great girl, and I'm proud that she's my daughter. I should tell her that more often.*

"Hey, Mom, I was just writing in my new journal that Aunt Teresa sent me. Did you have a job for me today?"

"Sure do, Silly. The people in 119 moved out a month ago, but they didn't leave a forwarding address, so their mail's piling up. Would you throw out the junk sale papers and dig up their phone number from the files? You know how that mail lady gets when a box is full. I'll put it on your tab."

"Mom! What's with you and this tab stuff? I work my fingers to the bone," Silly collapsed into giggles. This was just another fun benefit of 'working' for her mom. They would tease each other over pay and benefit packages all the time, laughing about 401ks and vacation time.

Rachel knew that Silly, ever prudent with her money, actually did have a savings account that most of her earnings went into every week. While it was a 'college fund' in name, Rachel knew that with Silly's brains, she'd receive scholarship offers galore, so Rachel hoped that she could talk Silly into a big trip with her friends, preferably after college, making memories she could enjoy for the rest of her life. She really was proud of that girl.

"When you finish up, would you find your brother and bring him to dinner? I know this won't take you long, and I'm almost done cooking. And Silly? I love you, my girl." Rachel was almost tearing up.

"Sure, Mom, love you too!" as Silly bounced off to handle her business.

Later that evening, as Silly loaded the dishwasher, she began to wonder what shape her life would take. The time for decisions was coming closer and closer, and she just couldn't make up her mind if she wanted to go to college here, or far, far away. She'd lived in the same area her whole life, and hadn't taken too many trips away. She couldn't know that she'd like it anywhere else in the world, so why would she commit to four whole years somewhere else? But still, adventure calls to the young with an ever forceful tone. College away might be grand and exciting, and worth missing her mom and Justin. But still, college was just a tool to hone her skills, the skills she'd been working on for nearly her entire life.

What Silly really wanted, more than anything else that had ever caught her fancy for more than a few minutes, was to be a famous author. Not just any old author, mind you, Silly wanted to write fairy tales that rivaled the infamy of the Brothers Grimm. She wanted to leave her mark on the world by changing children's' lives, by changing how they viewed the whole world around them.

Sure, Silly had had dreams of many other callings throughout her life, wanting to be a teacher, doctor, and astronaut at the ages when all the other kids wanted the same, but this was different. She'd begun telling her parents bedtime stories before she could even read, and one of the best memories she had was of her father listening intently one night before Silly went to sleep.

It had been a long, long story, full of witches and kings and horses and magical trees. The one regret Silly had in her life was that her parents had never recorded the stories she told back then, and her memory was full of their love, with not much room left over for the words she had shared with them every night.

Justin was a different story. After he was born, Silly had been a model big sister, practically nagging their mother to death to let Silly put the infant boy to bed and tell him stories. She remembered waking up in the middle of the night once, hearing her brother crying, and sneaking into his room before he could wake their mother so that she could finally be alone to tell him the stories she so loved.

It was when Silly finally worked out most of the kinks in her penmanship that she really began her life's work, albeit sporadically. She would write and write, but then the urge to record her stories would fade, and she would make them up in her head at night, before falling asleep, never committing a single word to paper for months. She wondered why she worked that way, but never really came to any conclusions, other than sometimes it felt right to write them down, and sometimes it felt right to simply think them, sharing with the rest of the world only through her dreams.

Her mind returned to the task at hand, briefly. The sink was almost empty, but she wanted this moment of Cinderella solitude to last just a bit longer. She tried to remember the very first story she told, but it was so long ago that she couldn't remember the details, only that there was a king and queen, and maybe a little prince? Oh well, she'd think more on that another time.

Silly returned to the question of college. Here or there? Near or far? Or maybe somewhere in the middle? Staying close to home would probably be her choice in the end, but she wondered where she could go, where she would go given the opportunity.

She stood, holding a plate, staring off into space. The whole world truly was her oyster at that moment. To stand at the entrance to the maze of life, full of hope and joy and an unmatched zest for absolutely everything. So many turns to take and choices to make, so many different paths to follow. Where could they all lead? It was a labyrinth that she would rejoice in solving, even if she never truly solved it. How many people realize, at such a young age, that the destination really is the journey?

This daze kept her in its warm embrace throughout the evening, that sense of 'all's right with the world' enfolding her. As Silly drifted off to sleep that night, she kept the smile on her face, and the story in her heart that had always begged to be told.

Three

The blaring alarm jolted Silly out of sleep the next morning. She lay a moment, wishing that school didn't have to be so early to be so much fun. Then, shaking off that mood, she flipped her covers back and swung her legs to the side to get up and face the new day.

After carefully choosing an outfit from her wardrobe, she completed her morning toilet and went to breakfast.

"Cereal again, or eggs today?" asked Rachel.

Silly replied, "I'll just fix myself some cereal yet again, mother dear."

Justin continued to chomp on his eggs and toast, absentmindedly kicking the leg of his chair in time with his chewing. A tiny smirk grew from one corner of his mouth as he realized what his foot was up to; he knew how much the kicking bothered both his mother and sister. A small annoyance, but he only took advantage of it when he was feeling especially mischievous, as he was this morning. A quick glance toward the kitchen showed Silly rolling her eyes, and he knew it was for him. The smirk grew just a smidge.

"What plans today, my little spawns?" Rachel smiled at her children, especially at the mischievous one. What he didn't know was that she secretly loved the chair abuse. It reminded her of their father. Since Justin didn't do it too often, it remained a sweet reminder, and not a painful wound that opened anew every morning at the breakfast table. She smiled a little more to herself, and then turned her attention back to the living.

Silly had shopping with Julia; Justin had exploring with Alex. He would be a filthy mess when he got home again tonight, Rachel knew, but she suffered through it. At least he was happy and knew better than to get into anything more dangerous than the small bit of woods on the lot next door. The simple joys of being a small boy! Rachel could only shake her head in envy.

Rachel kissed her two children goodbye as they finished packing up books and bags to be off to meet their separate school busses. The hours from 7:30 to 3 were always such quiet ones, compared to the boisterousness of after school fun and games. Even when she had a pile of applications to sort through, checking references, making callbacks, and sending Tony, the maintenance man, off on so-called emergencies. When would Mrs. Lawrence in 301 learn that her faucet would continue to drip if she didn't turn the water all the way off? Probably never, Rachel laughed to herself. She shook her head and waved out the front door.

Silly and Justin scampered out the door, poking at each other for the last few minutes before Silly's bus would arrive, usually right before Justin's.

Silly and Julia always sat together on the bus, ever since fourth grade when Julia had moved into the apartment complex. That had been their best summer ever. Silly remembered Julia looking so shy and lonely, watching the movers take all of her things from the truck into her new apartment. She'd watched from the window for a few minutes before asking Rachel if she could go introduce herself. Rachel had readily agreed, her hands quite full with a potty-training Justin.

Silly walked right up to Julia, who looked down at the ground between her feet when she saw a stranger coming right towards her; kid or not, strangers were Julia's biggest fear in life at that time. But who could resist this bouncing blonde girl with a name as silly as Silly? When Silly grabbed her hand, Julia didn't even hesitate to run right along behind her, learning where the pool was, where the nice and mean neighbors lived, which was the best bush to hide behind to listen to the Johnsons have their screaming fights that never quite graduated to blows. That last was quite a shock for Julia, whose parents never even raised their voices. But the obscenities this couple shouted at each other! It was grand fun, and so began what both girls knew would become a lifelong friendship.

But *this* morning there was something new. A new boy on the bus! He looked to be about their age. Maybe he'd be in one or more of their classes! Silly and Julia giggled together over his cute looks and brand-new outfit. When they arrived at school, he looked a bit unsure, so Silly pointed him in the direction of the office.

Wouldn't you know it, as soon as the morning announcements finished, into Silly's homeroom walked the new boy. He handed his card to the teacher, Mrs. Walter, who announced that Gregory Chase Baker was joining their class all the way from New York City. He glanced up at the class, then back down at his sneakers, mumbling that he went by Chase. Silly knew she'd get to know Chase. The only empty seat left was right behind hers, and they were already neighbors. He headed down the row to the empty seat, herded by the teacher and followed by the eyes of twenty-three other students. Mrs. Walter continued on to the supply closet, which she unlocked to remove one textbook, then relocked and placed the text gently on Chase's desk. When he didn't look up, she offered a glare to the rest of the class, who knew immediately that Mrs. Walter did not take kindly to her class ignoring the new kid.

Silly jumped right in and introduced herself. "I'm Silly, and yes, that's my name. It's nice to meet you, Chase."

Several other classmates announced themselves after that, and Mrs. Walter let them socialize for a few minutes before regaining everyone's attention at the front of the classroom.

"Class, let's give Chase a few days to acclimatize himself to his new surroundings. Our small town is going to be quite a change from New York, and there's no way he'll learn all of your names the first day! Let's learn some more biology."

The rest of the day breezed by for Silly, who couldn't get her mind off this new boy, Chase, who was really cute, and she could have sworn that he actually winked at her in the hallway after biology.

On the bus ride home, she told Julia, who hadn't had a chance to meet Chase. It was so unfair that the two friends couldn't have matching school schedules, or at least be on the same lunch shift. A whole day's worth of gossip had to be saved until the final bell at 2:20.

It was strange, though. Even though Silly knew that Chase had winked at her, he didn't even give her a first glance, let alone a second, either on the bus or after they all stepped off it. Chase walked straight down the corridor to his apartment, not letting Silly and Julia have a chance to admire him.

The girls headed towards Silly's apartment, since it was the closest, and dropped their schoolbags on the floor as soon as they went through the door. They reclined dramatically on the couch together, and then laughed at their own silliness.

"I can't stay too long," frowned Julia. "I forgot I have that biology test tomorrow that I really do need to study for. You can get away with not cracking a book outside of school, but you know I need to read it over and over before I really know it, at least well enough to pass a test." She sighed. "Sometimes life just isn't fair."

Silly put the back of her hand to her forehead, pretending to be so affected by the loss of quality time with her best friend. "My dear, whatever shall I do without you? It will be simply ages before I can see you again. I might pine away altogether. What sorrow is this life!" Silly peeked out from behind her hand to make sure that Julia was getting the full effect of her dramatic speech. "I just can't live without you, my darling!" But that part was just too much; Silly dropped her hand and burst into laughter.

Julia joined in, with not quite so much enthusiasm. After all, she did have that biology test. Julia sighed, and straightened her shoelace. "I can't wait to be done with school. It's not that it's really difficult, it's just so, well, tedious to read the same things over and over again. And you know as well as I do that neither of us is ever going to study biology in the real world. You'll be a famous author and I? I shall be the beautiful housewife who has servants to do all of her housework, nannies to take care of the children, and a handsome, fabulously wealthy husband."

Silly wasn't the only person in the room with a flair for the dramatic. Julia could definitely hold her own in that arena. It was often a sight to behold, the two of them competing to see who could be the most over-the-top in her speeches. As Silly's mother always said, at least it helped with their English compositions.

"Is it a quarter to four already? It feels like we've only been home a few minutes!" Julia pouted, as she gathered up the books that had spilled from her bag when she carelessly threw it on the floor in the entryway.

"It'll be summer soon, and then we can goof off all day, every day!" cheered Silly, optimistic as ever.

"Summer can't come soon enough for me. I can't wait to get back to swimming." Julia truly believed that she had been born human by mistake; she just knew she was really meant to be a sea otter, drifting along on a mat of seaweed, going wherever the currents led her, dining on fish and shellfish alike, whenever she got hungry. She sighed, and resigned herself to the short, dry walk to her apartment. "Bye, Silly. I'll call you later."

"Bye, Julia. Don't forget to take breaks from studying so hard!" Silly admonished her friend.

Julia rolled her eyes as she closed the door behind her. The teasing was all in good fun; the two had never hurt each others' feelings, not even accidentally.

Silly leaned her head back on the couch cushions and closed her eyes.

Four

Dear Diary,

I know it's only been a day since I've written to you, diary, but it's been one of two things I've been thinking about all day! What could possibly be the other, you ask? A boy. His name is Chase, but just between the two of us, I'm going to call him Alistair. That's such an aristocratic name, and I'd love to use a code name when I'm writing to you. Oh. What about posterity? Oh well! Don't forget that I'm still only fifteen, no matter how precocious I may be, and my name is Silly! I do like to be silly sometimes, just to earn my name.

Anyway, new boy. Alistair. The code name makes him seem so much more mysterious! He really is cute, and in my biology class. Sitting next to me! I wonder why his parents moved here from New York, especially in the middle of the school semester. That has to be so hard. I've been going to the same schools with the same group of kids since kindergarten, and I never even thought about how other kids have to do it, like the ones whose parents are in the military. I don't think I'd like moving around a lot, having to make new friends every year or so, having to leave all my old friends behind. I guess it would prepare you for being an adult, though. I wish people didn't have to move so much for so many reasons. It's probably easier on me and Justin that our dad died instead of our parents getting divorced. That's got to be harder, having parents and not being able to see both of them.

Julia and I could not stop speculating about Alistair today on the bus ride home. Maybe his family is in witness protection! Maybe they're fugitives from the law! Maybe his dad embezzled billions from his company and if his boss finds them his goons will kill the whole family! I know it's really nothing like that, maybe his parents just made their money and retired here or something as simple as that, but it's fun to make it so dramatic.

Once we get to know him, he'll be just like everybody else, right? Just another kid trying to make his way through high school. I'd better enjoy making stories up while I can before we find out the truth. The truth is always so boring! Well, most of the time.

It's funny that I had this grand plan of leaving my words for posterity to find them in a million years. Look at me, my second entry in this diary and I've already stopped with the sociology and moved on to fiction. I wonder what they'll make of that. I guess I'll never know, unless someone invents a time machine before I die!

I wonder where I'd go if I had a time machine. I mean, after I go introduce myself to my father. I hope he'd be proud of who I grew up to be. Mom says he would be, and she says that she's proud of me, but what if he would have changed over the years? I know people do that; you can never really predict the future, especially when it comes to people, even yourself. It would be nice to have a real answer, direct from the source. I really miss him sometimes, like now.

Sometimes I just get so angry that everyone else still has their dad, even if he doesn't live with them anymore. At least they know he's alive and can talk to him. I think I'm going down a bad road with this. I wish I could just wake up one morning and hear his voice, though. That would be nice. I miss my dad.

I'm going to bed now. I'm glad I wrote some about my dad, but I'm sad that this is the only way I can remember him, by making new memories of remembering him by myself instead of being with him and doing all that father/daughter stuff. Goodnight.

Five

The remainder of the school year went by too quickly for Silly. She and Julia went to class, hung out at each other's homes, and went shopping. The novelty of Chase had worn off quickly once they realized that he wasn't going to show interest in their timid advances. He did seem to play the field well and break more than one heart, so the girls soon understood that he wasn't their cup of tea. Silly certainly would have enjoyed a date or two with him, as would have Julia, but it wasn't worth becoming more fodder for the rumor mill.

As finals drew near, Silly realized that she hadn't written in her diary for weeks and weeks, but there were so many other practical demands on her time, she couldn't justify to herself cancelling any of her other obligations for flights of fancy. Silly's year-end grades came in top of her class, and Rachel took Silly and Justin out to dinner to celebrate her brilliant children.

The dinner out was a nice surprise for the kids. Rachel loved to stay at home and cook so that she could be sure she knew exactly what her children were eating, plus it helped her to stay within her monthly food budget. But she always had something set aside for special occasions, so that's what Rachel dipped into to pay for tonight's meal.

Silly was so excited that they were going out, she couldn't make up her mind what she would wear. After an hour trying different outfits and accessories, Rachel and Justin demanded that she simply go in what she had on right this minute. Silly sighed, frustrated that her family just couldn't understand how important outward appearance was to a teenage girl, but agreeably came out of her room in a simple t-shirt and jeans, with a beautiful amber necklace that had been a gift to her mother from her father on one of their first dates.

Silly treasured each and every piece of jewelry that her mother had passed down to her, especially the pieces that had been gifts from her father. It was another way Silly could feel close to him, although he was gone. That was something that was very important to Silly, and the whole reason that Rachel would so soon part with gifts that had such special meaning to her.

When Rachel saw the necklace, she smiled through the pain that she was feeling. It would have been so wonderful to be able to share these milestones with Dennis. She felt like she missed him so much more on special occasions. Sometimes Rachel would pretend that he was asleep in her bed at night, and she would tell him all the things she had never had a chance to say out loud before.

But tonight was a happy night, so Rachel put those thoughts aside to herd Justin to the car, with Silly following along behind the two of them.

"Well, my children, where shall we head to this evening? I was thinking pasta. How does that sound to you? Rachel asked as they all buckled up.

"Sounds good to me!" replied Silly, and Justin nodded enthusiastically.

"Well, garlic bread, here we come!" and Rachel headed off toward their favorite Italian restaurant.

The family sat down, and dug in when the server brought their appetizers of garlic bread and salad. Rachel thought about how it was so nice that someone else's kitchen was going to need the cleanup tonight.

All three of them decided on lasagna for dinner. When they'd cleaned their plates to the best of their ability, to-go boxes were called for and filled, and Rachel paid the check. The family packed everything up and headed for their car.

"Who's up for dessert? The ice cream shop is open for another half hour if anyone wants any," offered Rachel.

Seven

Unexpectedly, the longing crept back into Silly's heart and mind to reconnect with herself through her diary. However, Silly wondered sometimes if she was really cut out to be a writer, seeing as how she had abandoned her friend after only two entries.

One morning in June, she realized that it didn't have to be like that. She didn't have to abandon her dreams or her diary; she could pick it back up at any time. All it took was a few minutes and a pen. She vowed to herself to make this the summer of living dangerously. She would face her fears and conquer them. She would write and laugh and have fun.

That night, Silly went to bed with a smile on her face for the first time in a few weeks. It wasn't that the past weeks had been tiresome or troubling; they just hadn't been especially enjoyable. Things would be different now. Things would be exciting!

She planned to spend the rest of the summer working on her skill as a storyteller. She would have long, personal conversations with her diary and learn more about herself along the way. She would write down all those fairy tales that had been backed up in her mind for so long. Maybe she could even join some kind of summer reading program for kids at the library and read her fairy tales to preschoolers to see how they liked them. Justin had always loved her stories, and it would be nice to have a whole group of little kids to entertain.

This was going to be a lot of fun. She'd read, write, and hang out with Julia. What could possibly go wrong?

Silly was such an optimist sometimes.

Eight

Dear Diary,

I know it's been far too long since I've talked to you, my dear darling diary, and I promise to change that! I decided last night to make some changes in my life, and you're number one now. I will write in you at least three times a week. I would promise every day, but you and I both know that I'll never be able to keep up with that!

Can we start over? Can you find it in your heart to forgive me for abandoning you for all this time, never even opening your cover or turning your beautifully blank pages, dreaming of the magnificent words that will one day fill them? Can you possibly still love me?

As you can see, I'm still Silly. Ha! I'll always be Silly to you, diary. Do you like that you're almost a real person now, that I use your name? But that's not a name. I should give you a real name, shouldn't I? Like Alistair. Maybe not.

I'll tell you a little more about Alistair, since I did leave you hanging without ever telling you why his family really moved here.

Once upon a time, there was a king and a queen, and they wished for a baby. When the baby was finally born, it was a boy, and they decided to name him Alistair. The queen thought the name was perfectly lovely, and the king could never, ever disagree with his lovely bride, so Alistair it was. The king and queen watched with proud parent eyes as Alistair grew up, growing big and strong and smart as only princes can. But all was not well within the kingdom.

One day, the king fell ill, and the queen was beside herself with worry. She was so afraid that she would lose her king, and the kingdom would lose its leader, and Alistair his father. She tried every medicine that everyone in the kingdom suggested, but to no avail! It seemed that the king would surely perish after all, but finally, when the king was practically at death's door, a mysterious old woman showed up at the castle. She had a hunchback, and carried a large sack full of mystical potions and all the ingredients she needed to make as many more as she could sell.

The captain of the guard tried to send the old woman away because he thought she was a mere beggar, but the queen, with her good heart, stopped him. The queen brought the old woman to the kitchen to feed her well, and then personally escorted her to a room where she could rest. It was only then that the old woman revealed herself to be a true witch!

The queen was taken aback, and feared for her own life as well as her husband, the king's. But the witch laid her fears to rest as she explained that she had come down form the very tops of the icy mountains that made the boundary of the kingdom to the north. The witch had heard of the king's grave illness, and because she did not want any usurper to steal the throne and invade her precious icy mountains, she came to bring the cure.

The witch told the queen that she knew what ailed the king, and that she, and only she, knew the cure that he must have within the hour, or the king would die. The queen panicked, and asked if the witch would be able to have the cure ready in that meager amount of time. The witch assured her that yes, of course she would. This witch had powers that mere mortals cannot even imagine in their wildest dreams or darkest nightmares. The queen begged of the witch to please, make the cure, whatever the cost, she would pay.

The witch smiled to herself and sent the queen to the king's bedside, assuring the queen that she would attend with the cure well before the hour was gone. After the queen left the witch's room, Alistair peeked out from around the corner where he'd been hiding the entire time! The queen was so concerned for the king that she hadn't noticed

Alistair at all. The witch swept him into the room with her and slowly, menacingly, closed the door right in the faces of the shocked servants who saw that Alistair was in there with the witch, all alone.

The servants tried to listen through the door, but they could hear nothing. They tried to warn the queen, but she was too absorbed with worry for her husband, the king. What was really only a few minutes passed like hours, and finally, finally the witch creaked her door open again, but Alistair was nowhere to be found.

The witch made her way to the king's bedroom, where the guards blocked her way for only a second before the queen ordered them to let this woman pass.

The queen's relief at seeing the witch by the king's bedside was palpable, but still, the queen was a little uneasy to see the horrible murky shade of green that tinted the potion in the tiny glass vial that the witch tipped up and over to pour entirely into the king's mouth. Within seconds, his color was healthier, and less than a minute after he drank the mysterious brew, he leapt from his bed and kissed the queen soundly!

The witch saw this and threw her head back to laugh, so wickedly, and everyone in the room, who had begun to cheer for the king's return to health, fell silent. The witch pointed one long, bony finger at the royal couple, and their arms, which had clung to each other in joyful embrace, fell to their sides in utter confusion.

"Where is your son?" the witch asked of them both.

The king and queen fearfully looked into each other's eyes, and thought they knew the truth. The payment for the king's own life had been the life of his only son and heir!

The queen fell to the floor, wailing for Alistair. The king tried to storm towards the witch with his newly returned strength and health, but she simply put her hand up, and he froze in place.

"Yes, I have your son. He is mine forever, until and unless I decide otherwise. But listen! There is one thing that you can do to have him back."

"Anything!" cried the king and queen in unison, their voices mingling in their pain and grief.

"Anything?" mocked the witch.

"Please!!" they begged.

"Very well, my dears, I shall reunite you for all time," prmised the witch, and evil smile splitting her features.

The witch waved her hand, and the king and queen were no longer king and queen. They were no longer in their royal palace, or even in their kingdom. They were lost in the midst of some great, beautiful wilderness, but standing in front of them, seemingly unchanged, was Alistair! The pair reached for their son, but something in his eyes had changed. This was not the little boy that they had known and loved for all of his life. This was a monster.

As soon as they were within his reach, Alistair opened his new mouth full of great sharp teeth, and ate them both. His demon eyes roamed the new landscape, searching for his next victims. He was able to take any shape, and even form more than one person.

That's how he lives here with his 'parents.' They're just an extension of his form, and not real people at all. He ate all the alligators in the sewers of New York, and most of the homeless people who lived down there too. One smart police officer was catching on to him, so he decided to move here by throwing a sharp bone fragment at a map of the country.

Scary stuff, huh? Julia and I worked on it for ages, talking late at night over popcorn. It was more fun than staying up watching movies, for sure. We even drew pictures of the monster. I know I cut it off a bit short, but I didn't really plan for much after the climactic moment of Alistair eating his parents up. That was where my story ended. Julia actually contributed the tie-in between then and now. She insisted that I was the writer, but I talked her into contributing a little bit more than her complete attention. I'm glad I did, even if the new ending doesn't really fit with the rest of the story. Maybe I'll work on it more some other time.

Anyway! It turns out that Chase is a real jerk. He had six different girlfriends in the two months between when he got here and when school got out, and took advantage of all of them before dumping them and moving on to his next victim. So you see, he really is a monster, well, kind of. Bad enough for us not to like him, anyway. I'm just glad he didn't try to prey on me or Julia. Not that he could have conned us into doing it with him, but I'll bet that even if he hadn't, he still would have told everybody that he did. Like I said, a real jerk. I wish he weren't, though. He's still awfully cute. Why are all the worst guys so attractive?

Diary, like I said, I made a promise to you. Minimum three times a week, you and me, we got a date. Love ya! Bye.

Nine

The dreams came back that night, as they did nearly every night now, but this time with a vengeance. Ever since that night when the family had gone out to celebrate and returned home to that weird feeling of uneasiness, Silly's sleep had been nothing if not troubled.

This night, Rachel woke three times to the sound of Silly's moaning in fear. The third time, Rachel rose from her bed and walked down the hall. Just as she raised a hand to Silly's doorknob, the sweet sound of Silly's laughter bubbled from her room. Rachel heaved a sigh of relief, shook her head, and returned to her own comfortable bed.

Rachel should have opened the door. The laughter quickly turned to mumbling, then muffled screams. If Rachel had been in Silly's room, she would have found her daughter squeezing her pillow to her face in pain. These dreams were not just simple nightmares anymore. They almost felt real, almost left marks on Silly's skin. It wouldn't be much longer before they truly became real, in a way that neither Rachel nor Silly could ever have imagined.

But as of yet, Silly had no recollection of anything that happened while she was sleeping. She didn't remember her mother trying to shake her awake because she was so worried. She didn't remember the restless nights.

All Silly knew was that she was growing more and more tired during the day. She thought she was getting enough sleep; she was going to bed at her usual time and didn't have a problem going to sleep. She didn't wake up early or at all in the middle of the night. At least, not that she remembered.

Ten

June 9, 2012

Dear Diary,

Here I am, back again so soon! Did you miss me? I missed you. I wonder how I found time to miss you, since I went to bed after writing in you last night, and here I am first thing this morning! I had a great time sharing the story about the wicked witch with you. Maybe one day I'll publish my book of fairy stories, with beautiful illustrations by some talented artist who loves the stories and telling them as much as I do.

Do you think it's strange that I made Chase the focus of that story? There's just something about him. I know I don't see him hardly ever since school let out, but when I do, it's almost like watching a shadow walk by. If I weren't so attuned to his presence, I think I'd miss him. I don't know how to explain it so anyone else could understand. I don't really know how to explain so I understand. It's like he's an invisible magnet. He tries to pull me in, but when I go, there's no one there. It scares me sometimes. I worry about Julia and Justin. Not that he'd do anything sexual with Justin, more that he'd hurt Justin. I don't want anyone to get hurt, especially not the people I love. Something just isn't right about Chase. He doesn't really belong here, somehow. Not just at school, but in this world, if that makes any sense at all. Sometimes he seems so alien.

New subject! I'm getting goose bumps talking about this so early in the morning, before anyone else is awake. It's exciting news, diary! Julia's birthday is next week, and we're having a sleepover. It's just going to be the two of us, since she's so shy, but her parents are picking up loads of stuff for us to have a spa night together after dinner and cake and ice cream. Mud packs and bathrobes and nail polish, it's going to be so much fun! Neither of us has ever had a real live makeover, and her mom is taking us to the department store tomorrow to have one. I'm really excited, and I know Julia is, too.

I hope Julia loves the present I got for her. It's a beautiful wooden chest, big enough for the foot of her bed, where she can put anything she wants inside and use the top for a seat. My mom called it a hope chest. She said she had one when she was a little girl, but it wasn't nearly as beautiful as this one is. I found it at the flea market last weekend. There are all different colors of wood inlaid on the top in a checkerboard pattern, with flowers and vines winding all over it. I can't wait to see Julia's face when she finds it in her room on her birthday! It's waiting in Justin's room now, but when Julia's mom takes her to lunch and shopping on her birthday, her dad is going to move it right in. I've been pressing some flowers to put in there so it won't be just empty when she opens it, and it'll smell good. Don't you love surprises, diary? I do.

Okay, I think it's time to start getting dressed and ready to face the world another day. I do love writing to you, diary, but I don't want to waste any of the time I have with my family, knowing how easily they can be taken away from me.

Eleven

The weekend came, and Julia's mom made good on her promise to take the girls to get their first makeovers. It seemed to Rachel that breakfast was hardly over before Julia was knocking on their front door, come looking for Silly to visit for a while before they left. Rachel approved of Julia as a friend for Silly, but sometimes it seemed that those two got into more trouble than they knew what to do with. It wasn't that either girl was bad, things just seemed to happen to the pair, things that snowballed into a much huger mess than they first began as.

Rachel thought back to the time some mischievous kids, or possibly adults, for that matter, put some bubble bath into the hot tub. Silly and Julia had been the first to take notice, or at least, the first to report what they'd seen. Instead of listening to Rachel and waiting for the bubbles to die down, the girls scooped them all out and accidentally left a trail on their way to the storm drain, killing most of the shrubbery between the pool area and the parking lot. What a mess that had been! Rachel sighed. Sometimes good intentions didn't lead to the best outcomes.

At least they were going to be supervised today, Rachel thought with relief as she opened up the office to begin her brief weekend day. She had a bit of filing left to do, and then it was home to take care of the laundry that seemed to pile sky high no matter how hard she tried to keep up with it.

The makeovers went over without a hitch, and the girls merrily trotted around the rest of the day with an extra thick layer over their own natural beauty. All Rachel could do was shake her head at their innocence, and reminisce about the days when makeup was the most important thing in her life. This time was so precious, and she hoped both girls were getting every bit of enjoyment that they could out of their youth.

Rachel sighed to herself as she folded the clean, warm towels, fresh from the dryer, and then stood with the basket in her arms, remembering.

Dennis and Rachel had been high school sweethearts, never even looking at another boy or girl. They had both known from the start that they fit together in a way that even their grandparents, each set married over fifty years, couldn't even begin to understand. Their love was so new, yet seemed so old. It was almost like looking in a mirror when they looked in each others' eyes.

Wiping a tear from her eye, Rachel shook herself, and came back to the present. She knew the ache in her heart would never fully go away, but she loved it all the more for not letting her forget about the wonderful times she was able to have with Dennis before he was gone.

As she balanced the basket between her thigh and the wall to replace the towels in the linen closet, Rachel thought she heard a sound from Silly's room. She cocked her head to the side, listening intently, but Justin thundered down the hall, nearly trampling her in his haste.

"Boys will be boys," she muttered to herself, under her breath. "And one day that boy will boy himself into a broken bone, the way he rumbles around here." Rachel paused a moment to thank her lucky stars for the excellent medical insurance coverage provided by the property owners. Just because Justin hadn't done himself any major damage yet didn't mean it couldn't happen any day.

Twelve

The next few days passed as had the beginning of the summer, lazy days with lots of hanging out at the pool. Justin seemed to be spending a lot more time around the house than he usually did, which Rachel welcomed as he was a great help when he felt like it, but Silly wondered sometimes why he wasn't constantly in the woods like he had been every other summer since he could play outside by himself.

It didn't matter too much overall, as Silly spent all her time either with Julia or alone in her room, thinking up new fairy tales for her diary. She had slacked off a little bit on her writing, but she still spent a lot of time composing in her head. It was a fun way to pass the time, and if she forgot something before she wrote it down, it always came back to her at another time.

Finally, it was Julia's birthday. Silly couldn't spend any time with her best friend until dinnertime, but she spent most of the morning by herself, waiting for Julia to leave with her mom so that Silly could go get her birthday surprise ready. As Silly sat at her desk, pen poised over paper to begin her latest fairy tale, a story drifted up to the top of her mind that was unlike anything she'd ever written before.

Thirteen

Dear Diary,

I have a new, exciting story for you today! It just came to me, like a dream. I'm not sure how it turns out at the end yet, but I'll get it started here while I'm waiting for Julia.

Once upon a time, there was a beautiful princess. She lived in her castle with her parents, the king and queen, and her younger brother, the prince. They were all very happy together, and all of the subjects of the kingdom loved the princess very much. They were so pleased that one day she would become queen after her father passed away, because oftentimes, the new ruler wants to make a lot of changes in the kingdom, but the princess, they knew, would be just and fair, and treat all of her subjects with the respect that they deserved.

One day, as the princess was riding her horse in the forest surrounding the castle, she heard a strange noise coming from a nearby stand of trees. She pulled the horse up to a stop, and looked around without dismounting. There didn't seem to be anything around, but suddenly, a strange boy stepped out from behind the cluster of trees and smiled up at her. He looked very poor. His clothing was all rags and tatters, and he wasn't carrying any food or water or even a coat, and it was beginning to get cooler outside at night.

The princess introduced herself to the boy and asked him if he lived somewhere close. When she learned that the boy didn't have a home, she promptly invited him to come and stay at the castle. She helped him up on her horse behind her, and they rode away to the castle.

When they arrived, there was a huge hustle and bustle that had not been going on when the princess had left for her morning ride. She looked around for the possible cause, but nothing seemed out of the ordinary. She decided to stop and ask one of the castle guards, who was sure to know, as it affected his job when there were many people coming and going.

The guard seemed very relieved to see her, and explained that the problem was that the king and queen had reported that the prince was missing from his bed.

The princess became very upset at learning this, and dragged the strange boy along with her to the throne room, where she ran up to her parents to find out what she could about her brother, whether he was still missing or if they had any new information, and what she could do to help.

The king and queen were very happy to see their daughter, and gave her a great hug. They had feared that whoever had kidnapped the prince had searched the woods for the princess as well, since everyone knew that she went for a ride in the forest nearly every morning.

The king stopped his retelling of the morning as soon as he noticed the boy who was standing behind the princess. He demanded to know who this stranger was and what he was doing in the throne room.

The princess reassured her father that she had found him wandering alone in the woods, and that he had no family or home to return to, so she had brought him along to feed and clothe him, and perhaps find a loving family for him to stay with forever.

At this explanation, the king's worried face relaxed, and he sent for a guard to take the boy to the kitchen at once to have a meal. As soon as the guard appeared, however, he dropped to his knees in relief, as he recognized the strange boy as the prince himself! But why hadn't the king and queen ended the alarm? Why wasn't the royal family rejoicing? It took nearly all of the castle staff trooping by the throne and agreeing that this was indeed the lost prince to convince the king and queen.

The princess was shocked. She had been the one to find her brother, lost in the woods and dressed in rags? This was all very confusing. It was very strange indeed that only her family was taken in by the prince's unconventional appearance. And then there was the story that he had told her when she'd first met him in the forest; why hadn't the prince himself known who he was?

Once everyone was convinced, it was as though a veil had been lifted, and the prince and his family again knew him and his true story. Still, there was a blank spot in the prince's memory of the night before, and he couldn't recall one detail of how he had come to be in the forest instead of his own bed.

The king ended the call for alarm, and made sure everyone knew that the prince was home and safe and sound. As soon as the kingdom had returned to normal, the king called for a council of his wisest men and women, and especially those who had knowledge of magic. The consensus was that the royal family had been the victims of some magical prank, for lack of a better explanation. It seemed that all was back to normal, but time would tell.

That night, as the princess lay in her bed, she thought she would never be able to fall asleep for all of the questions that swirled around in her mind about the whole situation with her brother. She was wrong. As soon as she closed her eyes, she drifted off into dreamland.

But what strange dreams she had that night! The first one was simple. She sat in her dressing room, brushing her long, golden hair, when she looked down and saw a beautiful necklace lying on the floor next to her chair. When she bent down to pick it up, its shining gold temptation always seemed farther away that it looked. She couldn't get close enough to it to touch it, no matter how hard she tried, no matter how close she stepped to it. It was always just out of her reach. With one last leap, she thought she would be able to catch the necklace, but alas! It simply vanished.

That was the end of the first dream, and it left the princess puzzled when she woke in the middle of the night. She couldn't think of anything in her life that she was chasing but unable to capture. She was a princess; practically anything she'd ever wanted was hers as soon as she made a request.

Still puzzling over the meaning of her dream, the princess quickly fell back asleep, and slipped into a much darker world.

It was the same forest that she rode her horse in almost every morning, but this time, the princess was on foot, and running furiously. She looked down, and the hem of her beautiful gown was torn and muddy. Her lovely little slippers were worn through, and she was running on bare feet. She was momentarily confused about why she was running, but just then, she heard a loud roar from behind her!

The princess screamed in fright, and turned her head to see if she could locate whatever it was that was chasing her. She could only spare short glances, and they were minutes apart, but every time she checked, there was nothing there. She didn't let that stop her from running.

Faster and faster she ran and ran, until she came to a cliff that was nowhere in the real forest near the castle. The princess was so shocked that she was barely able to stop herself in time from running right off the edge. Her arms pinwheeled, but she didn't fall. She turned around, just in time to finally see the monster that had been chasing her through the entire forest.

It was a gigantic dark beast, as though it was shrouded in a shadow, though the sun was completely out, and not a cloud was in the sky. Its massive feet thundered across the ground as it closed in on her.

The princess couldn't make out any details behind the shadow that covered the monster, but she knew it was evil, and she knew it was coming to kill her. She turned her head left and right, but there were no escape routes available to her at the very edge of this cliff. Its hot, steamy breath warmed her faced as it slowed to a crawl, and stopped only a few inches from her.

As she opened her mouth to scream, the shadow fell away from the monster's face, and she saw that it had the head of a bull. It opened its mouth once more to roar at her, and she tumbled backwards, falling from the edge of the cliff. She fell and fell, but never hit the ground.

When the king and queen went to check on the princess the next morning, they were unable to wake her up. They knew it was some kind of evil magic, but all the wizards in that kingdom and the surrounding areas were unable to break the spell.

The princess lived out the rest of her days in her bed, asleep, falling endlessly.

Fourteen

Silly dropped her pen and wondered at what she had written. This was the most personally disturbing story that she'd ever put to paper. She shivered, and looked at the clock. All of her anxiety about the story dropped away as she realized it was nearly time for Julia to be home! Silly quickly packed up her diary and pens and hopped up from her desk to finish getting dressed.

Earlier that day, Silly had been practically pacing in her anxiety for Julia to come home from her birthday expedition with her mother. Julia's dad had already come and gone with the chest, and Silly had supervised the meticulous placement of her dried flowers in the bottom on top of a piece of satiny material she'd found.

As Silly rushed to Julia's apartment to wait somewhat more patiently for her best friend to get home, she tripped and sprawled herself across the sidewalk. When she got up, she sheepishly glanced around to make sure that there were no witnesses, and she caught a glimpse of Chase quickly retreating around the corner behind her. Well, if he could find it in himself to pretend that nothing happened, she could too. Silly sighed with relief. She brushed herself off and continued on her merry way, greeting Julia's dad as he let her in to hide in their apartment.

Just then, Silly heard the familiar sound of Julia's front door squeaking open. She leapt up and raced around the corner to hide in Julia's parents' room to be ready to jump out and witness Julia's reaction as soon as Julia entered her room to see the chest. Silly was so excited she could barely keep quiet. She heard Julia's dad greet her and invite her to see if anything was new around the house...maybe in her room.

Julia ran down the hall to her bedroom, and squealed in delight just as Silly popped back around the corner. The two girls grabbed each other and jumped up and down in sheer joy. Silly was so happy that Julia loved her gift, and Julia was so happy that Silly gave it. They bounced over to the bed and fell over in their excitement, but immediately began planning what could go in such a lovely item.

Julia finally decided on storing blankets in it, for now, but only freshly scented ones, and she'd of course distribute the dried flowers evenly between them so that there would be a lovely floral surprise in every layer. Silly agreed wholeheartedly.

The best friends finally began to calm down, and realized that Silly had to go home right away to pack her overnight bag for their spa sleepover. In her mad rush, Silly hadn't brought a thing with her. Neither could wait to get started and see what goodies Julia's parents had lined up for them. After a quick hug, Silly left Julia's home, a skip in her step.

While prancing back to her own apartment, Silly caught a quick glimpse of someone sneaking off into the woods in the next lot. She shook her head, assuming that it was only her brother, Justin, off on another wild goose chase with one of his friends from school. He played in those woods all the time!

Silly remembered being nine years old and doing the exact same thing with Julia. They'd bring a blanket and pretend to have tea parties with the woods fairies. They'd climb trees and pretend they were Rapunzel, letting down their hair for princes to climb up and rescue them. Even when one of them was sick or busy, the other would bring a book to read while sitting under one of the great old trees.

Silly hoped no one ever decided to buy that land and tear those trees from the ground. It would be like losing a part of her childhood forever. It was always so hard for Silly to adapt to changes in the landscape of her life. She recognized that in herself, and understood that it probably came from the drastic change of losing her father at such a young age.

All of the inner contemplation had slowed Silly's progress down to a crawl. She snapped back to the present and saw that she was only a few feet from her own door, where her brother was peeking out to see if she was home yet. Justin had been pretty excited about Julia's surprise, and had been waiting anxiously for Silly to show up and tell him the details of whether Julia liked it or not.

When Silly walked in the door, she pretended to not even notice Justin, who rolled his eyes and reached out a foot to try to trip her. She hopped nimbly over his extended leg to plop down on the couch with a grin.

"She loved it!" Silly told Justin.

"Of course she did! I told you she would. You were so worried over nothing at all, Silly goose!" taunted Justin, using the name that always drove his sister up the wall. He laughed, and collapsed on the couch next to her. Silly reached out to tickle him, but changed her mind at the last instant and stood up instead.

"I've got to go get my stuff together for Julia's tonight. See ya later, little bro!"

Justin hated being called 'little bro' almost as much as Silly hated being called a goose, so he chased Silly all the way to her room, where she nearly took his fingers off by slamming the door just as he arrived.

"Enough already, kids!" hollered Rachel from the kitchen, where she was putting the finishing touches on the meatloaf that she and Justin would have for dinner that night, since they would be dining alone.

Silly stuck her head back out of her room long enough to chime in with Justin, "yes, Mother dear!"

As Silly was about to return to her packing frenzy, she remembered something, and called to Justin, "hey, I thought you were in the woods, not waiting on me in the living room. I could have sworn I saw you on my way home."

"Not me, Silly. None of us have been going in the woods for the past few weeks. There's something weird going on in there. You know I don't scare easy, but I won't even go into the woods with a whole group of people, and I'm definitely not going in there all by myself."

Silly stopped, confused. Hadn't she seen boys coming and going to and from the woods all summer? Now that she really thought about it, she hadn't seen anyone that she recognized. Usually only kids from the apartment complex played over there because there were no other neighborhoods close enough to make the trip worthwhile, especially when there were so many real parks between here and there. She started to say so to Justin, then remembered the one person she had recognized coming from the woods. Alistair. No, Chase. His real name was Chase. She would have laughed at her own confusion, but a chill went down her spine.

"That's a really good idea, Justin. I don't think any of us should go over there anymore, but most of all, I don't think anyone at all should go there alone anymore."

Justin looked up at his sister's now-pale face, and nodded. He didn't usually let her try to boss him around, but this wasn't your regular bossing. This was real concern, and Justin knew to acknowledge it for what it was. Silly loved him and didn't ever want to see him hurt.

"Do you think we should talk to Mom about it?" he asked.

"What do we have to tell her? I mean, there isn't any proof that anything bad happened, is there? Did you or any of your friends see anything?"

"Not exactly," fudged Justin, fidgeting with a button on his shirt. "It's just this feeling we all got, not together, but at different times. Everybody felt it, though. That's why we don't go there anymore. It feels bad, Silly. It feels evil."

"Mom would think we're crazy. Just help me make sure nobody goes there, okay?" Silly was still a little too preoccupied to notice the telltale signs that Justin wasn't being exactly truthful.

Justin agreed with relief, and, somber now, went down the hall to his own room.

Silly turned back and resumed gathering her things, but definitely not with the same exuberance with which she had begun. She didn't take long, and as she finished, closing her door behind her, she whispered in the direction of Justin's room, "I love you, Justin, be careful."

Rachel heard Silly coming down the hallway, and stood up from where she'd just sat down at the kitchen table to give her only daughter a hug. Rachel wondered why she felt so apprehensive. It was only one night, after all, and only at Julia's, on top of that. She'd lost count of how many times Silly had slept over at her best friend's apartment. Surely thousands of nights, by now. Even so, something wasn't right today. Something felt...evil? Was she really thinking that anything could possibly happen to Silly that would qualify as truly evil? Rachel told herself that she'd better get a good night's sleep tonight. Too much stress was putting crazy thoughts in her head. Too much worry about Silly not getting enough sleep.

"I love you, Sil; don't stay up too late giggling with Julia. And don't forget to tell her I said happy birthday," reminded Rachel, holding out her arms for a hug goodbye.

"I won't, Mom! And I will! And I love you, too!" Silly accepted the hug, returning it and giving her mother a swift peck on the cheek. "I love you a lot, Mom. I'll be home tomorrow."

Rachel closed the door behind Silly, and called to Justin to come out for dinner. He thumped out of his room and took his usual seat at the table.

"Oh, no, you don't, young man, your sister's gone, so you'll have to help me set the table tonight!" she grinned at Justin's dismay. "Why don't you get the good plates and real glasses, and we'll have a fancy dinner, just the two of us?"

With a smile for his mother, Justin rose from his seat and obediently went into the kitchen to retrieve the requested place settings. Then, just to get a reaction, he hid the plates on Silly's chair and put the paper plates he'd stashed between the real ones at his and his mother's seat. As she came out of the kitchen, both hands full of meatloaf and mashed potatoes, she sighed in exasperation with his mischief.

"Go get the gravy and green beans, goose, before I kick that little butt!"

Justin laughed at his own cleverness and ran to fetch the rest of dinner. He retrieved the plates from their hiding place, and smiled with his mom. They sat down and began to eat in companionable silence.

"What were you and Silly having such a serious conversation about before she left, Justin? I could only hear your tones, not what you were saying, but it sounded like it was pretty important." Rachel asked, looking her son in the eyes.

Justin paused for a long moment, casting his eyes downward toward the table, before deciding on his answer. "Well, we were talking about whether or not to talk to you, Mom. Silly noticed that me and my friends don't go to the woods anymore; it's just strangers playing in there now. I told her that we didn't go there anymore because, well, it doesn't feel right."

Rachel furrowed her brow at his answer. That was certainly not what she expected to hear, but it actually coincided with her own recent feelings when she looked out her office window at the woods. They looked the same as they always had, but there was something wrong. Something menacing. She realized the truth in what Justin was telling her; that it had been a long time since she'd seen anyone she knew playing out there. They were all new kids, and she hadn't rented to that many new families this whole year.

With a serious face, she responded to Justin. "Silly's an observant girl. I hadn't realized until you told me this that you don't talk about the woods anymore. I think you're absolutely right in your decision not to go there. I can't put my finger on what's been bothering me about the woods, but you're definitely right. It's not a good idea to go over there. I haven't," Rachel stopped herself. It wouldn't be a happy mealtime conversation to talk about kidnappings and murder. She knew Justin was a reasonable boy, and Silly was a reasonable girl, and they could keep themselves out of reasonable trouble, but still.

"Mom, you have that look. Don't worry, I'm okay. I don't take rides and candy from strangers, and I don't play in the woods anymore." Justin knew his mother's moods, and this was the face she got when she started to worry about things beyond her control. "I'm okay," he reiterated.

Rachel's eyes snapped back into focus, and she tried to smile at Justin. "I know, but you know how mothers are, we worry about our kids." She tried to play it off as normal concern for his wellbeing, but he saw through that.

"Mom, really. I think, if it would make you feel better, I wouldn't mind staying inside for a few days. I can just read some of my books and play some of my games. Nobody even has to come over. It hasn't been the same this summer, anyway, with so many of my old friends gone because they moved to real houses." Justin tried to reassure her, but he knew he was trying to reassure himself just as much. He didn't really want to leave. It was safer staying at home. Justin didn't know how he knew that, he just knew.

"I would like that. We could play your games together; maybe even talk Silly into hanging out a home a little bit more than usual." Rachel's mood began to lighten as she relaxed into the idea of her children being safely within her sight for a while. Then she laughed. "Do you think I'm just being silly old mom, scared of my own shadow?"

"I really don't. Something isn't right, but for once, I don't want to be the one to find out exactly what it is. I'd be okay with never finding out, as long as it just goes away. That would be a happy enough ending for me." Justin resumed shoveling the food in his mouth with barely a pause to breathe, his usual method of eating.

"Slow down enough to taste it!" chastised Rachel, and all was back to normal between them, the serious conversation out of sight, out of mind. For now, at least.

Fifteen

Silly showed up at Julia's door, not out of breath as usual, but calm and quiet. Julia's mother wondered what was wrong as soon as she opened the door. Something in Silly's eyes told her not to push the issue, but to leave it until Silly was ready to talk about it. She went back into the kitchen, where she and Julia's dad were finishing up dinner for the four of them.

When Silly got to Julia's room, she snuck up behind Julia and put her hands over Julia's eyes.

"Guess who!"

Julia laughed, and squirmed out of Silly's reach. "I waited for you to get back to open the bag of goodies my dad got us! Let's check it out."

They dug into the goody bag with so much vigor, they were lucky it was cloth. Paper would never have stood up to the abuse the two were dishing out in their hurry to display everything contained therein. After minutes on end of gasps, giggles, and sighs of admiration, the bounty was displayed across Julia's bed.

"We are so lucky! Just look at all this stuff, lotion, foot scrub, four colors of nail polish with remover, facial scrubs, gel masks, eye masks, cooling lotions, and even these cute cotton slippers to wear! This is going to be the best birthday ever!" crowed Julia, her eyes shining with excitement.

"This is so awesome, you're right! Let's go tell your parents how much we appreciate all this, and then start making a huge mess," grinned Silly, always up for some fun.

Just then, Julia's mom called the girls to dinner. The four of them sat down to a beautifully set table complete with stemware and candles. It was Julia's favorite grotesquely fattening dish, batter-fried pork chops and home made French fries. There was a freshly tossed garden salad to make a nod towards health consciousness, but since the family rarely ate anything that wasn't good for them, Julia's parents didn't bother arguing with Julia about her own birthday dinner.

The family and their guest made small talk about the girls' coming junior year of high school and what possible plans they had made for their lives, but most of the sounds coming from the dining room were chewing and moans of delight in the meal.

"Don't stuff yourselves too much; we've still got cake and ice cream to eat! And a whole load of snacks, because I know you two will be up all night having fun, as usual." Julia's mother had a mockingly stern look on her face that dissolved into a grin as Julia's jaw dropped upon hearing her mom's tone of voice.

Everyone laughed and pitched in to clear the table for the beautifully moist yellow cake covered in rich buttercream frosting. Julia's parents had carefully placed sixteen candles on top, and Silly dimmed the lights as they began to sing 'Happy Birthday' to Julia. With a great inhale, Julia blew out the candles and squeezed her eyes shut tight.

"What did you wish for?" teased Silly, who knew her superstitious best friend would never share a wish made before it came true.

As always, Julia smiled mysteriously and replied, "World peace, of course," and sliced the cake, setting each piece gently on one of their glass dessert plates as her father dished out bowls of vanilla bean ice cream.

"That's my plain old vanilla ice cream girl, nothing but traditional for you, right?" he smiled at Julia. "Not even chocolate."

"That's right!" she readily agreed. Then, "Mom, I don't know why you never opened a bakery! This is the most beautiful and yummy cake I've ever had in my life!" praised Julia. Silly, her mouth full, nodded enthusiastically in agreement. Silly's praise came out too muffled to understand, as she'd taken a huge first bite, having already known of Julia's mother's prowess in the kitchen, especially when it came to baked goods.

Then all conversation ceased, as everyone settled in to savor every last crumb of Julia's wonderful birthday cake. When no one could take another bite, all plates were pushed back, forks laid on top, and butts scooted down just the tiniest bit in their chairs. It had been a lovely dinner, and Julia's eyes shone with the promise of many, many more birthday dinners with the same friend and family.

Julia smiled contentedly to herself, and heaved a sigh, breathing the sentiment of 'all's right with the world.' Her parents glanced at each other in appreciation of the amazing child they had raised through adolescence, and Silly was glad to feel the joy in her heart that she had made such a wonderful friend.

"All right, girls, if you can roll yourselves out of the dining room, we'll clean up in here. And, surprise! We're even going over to a friend's house for the rest of the evening, so you'll be home alone and free to scream and giggle as loudly as you want until the wee hours." Julia's mom gave her dad a knowing look, and they slowly stood up and began to gather the remains of the dessert feast.

Silly laughed out loud. "Us making noise? Whatever can you be thinking?" Julia joined Silly in the laughter, and then thanked her parents for making this such a great sixteenth birthday.

"You know this was absolutely perfect. I wouldn't want anything but this. Who needs all that craziness you see on TV? Dad, you're right. Plain old vanilla ice cream, that's me!" Julia truly was happy.

Both girls left their places at the table and made their way back to Julia's room to gloat again over the bounty of spa-related products that lay spread out before them. It was a girl's dream come true. There were facial scrubs, and peppermint foot scrubs, and three different lotions, and five different shades of nail polish, and shower caps for their hair, and fresh white terry cloth bathrobes to swaddle themselves in.

"Where should we start?" asked Silly. "It's your birthday, after all. You set the schedule."

Julia's smiled widened as she looked up at her friend. "Let's do feet first, then faces, then take a movie break and decide what else. Does that sound good to you?"

"Sounds fantastic!" replied Silly, a gleam in her eye.

Julia's parents stopped in the doorway to offer their goodbyes for the evening, and the girls thanked them one more time for their generosity. With a last glance back, the adults left the two teenagers to their own devices.

Silly peeked around the corner to make sure they were really gone, and squealed with delight that they were. Sure, Julia's parents were way cooler than most, but still, adults around versus no adults? That's not even a question.

They each snagged a bathrobe, and Silly headed to Julia's bathroom, while Julia made a beeline for her parents' much larger master bath. A short while later, each emerged, hair wrapped in a soft, fluffy towel, body wrapped in a soft, fluffy robe.

Silly grabbed a fresh towel from the linen closet, and brought it to the living room, where Julia was waiting with the peppermint foot scrub.

"Okay, birthday girl, you first!" Silly sat on one end of the couch and waited for Julia to take the other and swing her feet up into Silly's lap. Silly opened the bottle and began to massage the heavily scented lotion into Julia's feet. When she was finished, Julia swung her feet to the floor, and Silly threw her feet into Julia's lap for the same treatment.

After Silly's feet were done, the girls laughed and wiggled their toes in sheer pleasure. They leaned back into the couch cushions to enjoy the minty tingling in their feet for a few more minutes before jumping up to head back to the master bathroom, which had two sinks, one for each of them to use when applying their face masks.

Silly opted for the moisturizing pack, while Julia went with the refreshing cucumber peel. They made silly faces at each other in the mirror during their applications, and returned to the couch to listen to some music while the masks dried.

Julia surfed through the radio stations until she found a song she liked, which made her grab Silly to jump up and dance. Dancing is twice as much fun when you've just had a foot massage, and even better when it's your birthday and you're home alone with your best friend.

Eventually it was time to wash their faces, and both girls were pleased to note that neither had left any funny residue on their clean faces.

It was still pretty early, so Julia picked a movie for the two of them to watch while they painted their nails. After a long debate with herself, she chose a romantic comedy that they'd already seen a million times, but still loved. Silly agreed that it was the perfect choice, since they wouldn't be able to pay that much attention to what was going on on the screen while they were painting and polishing.

Silly chose to paint her toenails a shimmery purple polish, while Julia decided to stick with a classic dark red. After two coats, however, Silly's toes looked like they'd been badly butchered with a hacksaw.

"This color's nothing like it looked in the bottle! Don't you hate when that happens? I think I'll start over with that blue. Did you bring the cotton pads and nail polish remover, Julia?"

Julia hadn't, so Silly hobbled her way back to Julia's bedroom, where she had to dig around in Julia's makeup bag, finally deciding to just dump the whole thing out on Julia's desk since she couldn't find any remover inside. And there it was, the very last thing that fell out of the bag. Silly scooped it up as she realized that there was a brand new bottle in the goody bag and groaned to herself in consternation. She shook her head as she left the room and stopped to fetch some cotton pads out of the medicine cabinet. By the time she made it back to the living room, Julia had finished with her own toes, and offered to take care of Silly's.

"Thank you! You know I'm horrible at painting my own toenails. I always get polish so far up my foot it's almost like I took a bath in it! Okay, okay, I'm exaggerating. But not much!"

Julia laughed and nodded. "No offense, but I do know. I don't know what happened to your beauty sense. Maybe you were just born without one, and will have to take lessons or depend on salons for the rest of your life!"

Silly hung her head at the truth. She had never, ever been able to get the hang of nail polish. Even worse was eyeliner. She'd lost count of how many hours and hours she'd spent staring into the bathroom mirror, concentrating so hard her tongue stuck out, only to end up with a black mess around her eyes. Julia alone knew the real reason Silly never wore eyeliner: she hated the complicated stuff, and couldn't trace around her eyelid to save her life.

Silly didn't care; she knew Julia would keep her secret. That's what friends were for. If you couldn't let on to your best friend that you were a hopeless case with eyeliner and nail polish, it was time to find a new best friend.

Silly watched as Julia concentrated on painting Silly's toenails, being careful not to spread polish onto her skin. Some people could achieve amazing things with practice, including Silly, but staying inside the lines with nail polish was just not one of them.

The blue turned out much better than the purple had, and Silly and Julia were both pleased with the shimmery effect. With the spacers still between their toes, the girls kicked their feet straight out and admired their new paint jobs.

"How about we pop some popcorn in the microwave and start the movie over? I haven't watched it with my full attention in ages, and I don't think you have either. We haven't even been saying the lines along with it, and I don't know if I even remember them all anymore!" suggested Julia. The sparkle was back in her eyes, and at Silly's nod, Julia jumped up to run to the kitchen, completely forgetting about her toenails.

Silly gasped, and then laughed. "My mom's going to kill you for staining up this carpet, Julia!"

Julia looked at the floor behind her, and groaned to see the dotted red trail in the pile of the carpet. "Oh, no!" she cried. "What am I going to do? Will the remover take it out or would that mess up the carpet worse?"

Silly reassured her friend. "Don't worry, it happens. And the remover will take it out just fine. Just be careful on your way back, and I'll start working to clean this up. It's a lot easier if you can get to it before it dries."

Julia visibly relaxed, her shoulders drooping down a bit as she recovered from her moment of panic.

"Don't they say something like every party has its problem? This was ours, and it's not even a bad one. Way better than burnt popcorn!" called Silly, as Julia turned around to continue toward the kitchen.

Julia giggled, claiming indignantly, "I never burn popcorn!"

Just then, there was a knock at the front door. Julia popped her head around the corner to look at Silly, who was just as confused. They weren't expecting anyone, and Julia's parents had keys, of course.

Silly got up and carefully walked to the front door, making sure her toes stayed up, since they weren't quite dry yet. When she looked through the peephole, she couldn't see anyone there. Silly sighed, shrugged, and headed back to her drudgery of cleaning the nail polish off the carpet.

"Just some kids knocking on doors as they go by, I'll bet," she told Julia. "If they keep it up, we'll just keep a lookout at the window so we can scare them into behaving."

Silly bent her head back down to her work as Julia resumed opening and closing cabinet doors, searching for the popcorn seasonings. Julia was a purist, favoring a sprinkling of salt with light butter, while Silly loved to mix and match whatever she could find to try new flavor combinations.

"Oh, my mom picked up some of that nacho cheese flavored popcorn shake-on stuff, did you want to try some of that?" she asked Silly.

Silly briefly considered, then agreed that maybe it was time she stopped complicating something as simple as eating popcorn. "Sure, I'll just go with the one flavor tonight." She grinned, pleased with herself for making such a sacrifice. "You'll have to be the one to tell my mom, though. She'll never believe it coming from my mouth!"

Julia conceded that with Silly's extravagant popcorn-topping history, her mother would certainly not believe Silly telling her such a thing.

There was another knock at the front door, this one a little louder.

Silly grumbled, "I am just not a fan of anyone going door-to-door annoying people. I mean, really, it's not nice. It's one thing for salesmen to do it, at least it's their job, but when it's just for a prank that's mean. There's an old lady in the next building who can barely make it to the door with her walker. What if she fell down because somebody knocked on her door and took off? Who knows how long it would be before she could get help?"

Julia wholeheartedly agreed. Her grandmother had broken a hip while at home alone, and had waited for hours until, fortunately, her letter carrier brought a package to the door and heard her calling. "You're right, Silly. I'll see if I can catch them running off."

But whoever it was had already made it out of sight, and after Julia checked the peephole, unlocked the door, and opened it, all she saw was an empty corridor. She shook her head and closed the door, locking it again behind her. Julia took a few steps to the side and adjusted the curtain on the front window a bit.

"Maybe they'll think someone's watching now, and will leave us alone for the rest of the night," Julia thought aloud.

"I hope so," replied Silly.

At that minute, the microwave beeped, announcing that the popcorn was ready for consumption, as long as they didn't mind their mouths being burned beyond recognition. Julia returned to the kitchen once again, and divided the bag of popcorn into two bowls. She salted and buttered her own bowl, and then brought the other bowl with the nacho cheese seasoning into the living room for Silly.

"Thank you for taking care of that carpet, Silly. I don't know what I was thinking. I really do appreciate it, though." Julia said.

"Julia, it's your birthday. And you know my mom wouldn't have really been that upset about it anyway, any other apartment and I'd be cleaning it up months after it dried and the tenants moved out. I'm just getting a head start. Aww, now I'm thinking about you moving away, and that would just be too sad for words!" Silly began to tear up at the thought of losing her dearest friend.

"Silly! My parents would never move away from here, would they? Oh no, now I'm sad too. What have we done to this poor little party?" cried Julia.

Silly had made it back to the couch, and was holding her bowl of popcorn, nacho cheese shaker in hand. "Let's just forget I ever said anything. Next thing you know we'll be talking about our weddings and moving off for college and having babies, and then we'll really be old!"

Julia laughed, and heaved a sigh of relief. "I'm glad you can always cheer me up, even when it was you who made me sad in the first place. Maybe I mean especially when it was you in the first place? Anyway, you're right. I'll start the movie over, and hopefully we can watch it in peace, with nobody banging on the door!"

As they adjusted their legs and feet on the couch while trying to balance their bowls of popcorn, Julia dropped the remote in the couch cushions. While digging around for it, she came up with a necklace. Julia twined the chain she felt around her fingers and lifted her hand to reveal the treasure she'd found.

"Oh, my," Julia whispered to herself, barely audibly.

Silly turned her head to see what had distracted Julia so much, and her mouth dried up at her first glimpse of the thing that would haunt her dreams.

"Is this yours, Silly? I know it isn't mine or my mom's. I've never seen you wear any jewelry with a stone this color, but it's kind of unique, and that's definitely your style!"

Silly took the necklace, and examined the pendant. "It's not mine, but it really looks familiar. Are you sure it's not your mom's? I know I've seen this design somewhere before."

It was a fine gold chain, closed with a regular lobster clasp, but the pendant was something special. It had a deep red stone in the center of what could be a stylized eye, or maybe a flower. Golden and silver wire wrapped around the stone in a widening spiral as it went from being thin, round wire to flat and smooth. The whole thing was smaller than a dime, but very finely crafted. The different colored wires looked thinner than a hair where they began to spiral from the red stone.

"You're right, Silly, it does look familiar. I can't think of where I would have seen it before, though. The chain is so short; it looks like a choker or a child's necklace. It's a mystery to me," claimed Julia.

"It's so pretty, and fascinating, the spiral looks like it goes in and in forever, so beautiful," Silly's voice trailed off. Silly's head began to nod, bobbing down and up as though she were trying not to fall asleep.

"Silly? Are you okay?" Julia's concern came out in the tone of her voice. "Are you hypnotized? Wake up!" She reached out to grab Silly's arm and shake her a bit, to snap her out of it, but stopped when she saw the strange look in Silly's eyes.

It was like looking into the eyes of the oldest person in the world. Silly seemed to be watching everything, and nothing, at the same time. She wasn't looking at Julia, she was looking through Julia, and it scared Julia like nothing else ever had. It almost looked as if...as if Silly weren't even there anymore.

Julia stood up from the couch and took a step back. The popcorn bowl slipped from her grip and fell to the floor, scattering kernels everywhere. Julia didn't even notice the mess, or that she'd dropped anything at all. She took another step back as Silly's head slowly turned to face her.

"What happened? Where am I? Julia?" Silly was talking in her own voice, but it sounded so far away, and muffled like she was in another room.

Julia took a deep breath and opened her mouth to reply just as Silly's hand jerked, and the necklace, with the pendant, dropped to the cushion next to her.

"What are you doing? I thought we were going to watch the movie?" asked Silly, completely back to normal, as if nothing had happened.

"I-I couldn't find the remote, so I was going to start it from the DVD player," stuttered Julia, totally at a loss as to what had just happened. Did she imagine the whole thing?

Silly looked down at the couch cushion next to her and saw the necklace. "What-"

"Don't touch it!" screamed Julia, launching herself toward the couch to snatch the necklace up before Silly could get a finger near it. Julia threw the necklace away from herself as soon as she scooped it up, and it landed in a small pile next to the front window.

"What was that about? What's wrong?" asked Silly.

Julia sank to the floor, trembling. "I don't know, Silly. I really don't know what's going on right now. Don't you remember me finding that necklace in the couch? Do you remember taking it from me to look at it? Do you remember anything?"

Fear crept into Silly's face as Julia's words sank in. "I don't remember ever seeing that necklace before. What are you talking about?"

Julia began to explain. "I dropped the remote in the couch, so I was digging around for it. I found that necklace instead. When I showed you, and you picked it up, you got...strange. You looked like you were a million miles away, like you were hypnotized, or like you were possessed. I don't know what to do right now, Silly, I'm really scared. Please just tell me you're playing with me. Please tell me this is some kind of joke."

Silly was shocked. "Julia, I really, truly, don't remember any of that. I'm not joking. Are you serious? Am I going crazy?"

Julia sat down on the couch close to Silly and took her hands. "Silly, we've been friends for a long time, and we're closer than just about anyone else I can even think of. Whatever's going on, we will get to the bottom of it. We will figure it out, and everything will be okay. I promise you that."

Silly nodded, biting her lip and fighting back tears. She had never before experienced anything like this. She had no idea what to do in a situation she had no memory of. Obviously, she and Julia were good girls, and didn't even associate with other teens who drank or did drugs. Neither had any experience with blackouts of any kind.

"Julia, what did I do? I mean, when I wasn't me." Silly wasn't sure if she really wanted the answer to this question, but she couldn't help asking.

"You just said something like the necklace was pretty, and you were following the spiral, or something. And then you were just gone. You didn't say anything else; you just looked at me, or through me. Are you sure you don't remember seeing anything?" asked Julia.

"I think…I think I remember feeling like something was pulling me. Taking me away to somewhere I didn't want to go. Somewhere dark and far away. Somewhere with—"Silly broke off, afraid to say the next word out loud.

"Where, Silly? It's okay, you know you can tell me anything," pleaded Julia.

"Somewhere with demons," finished Silly, unable to meet Julia's eyes.

Sixteen

Rachel woke with a start, sitting straight up in her bed. Something was wrong. Something was very wrong. She threw the covers to the side and leapt out of bed, running to Justin's room to check on him. She opened the door, fearing the worst.

And Justin was peacefully asleep, warm and safe in his own bed.

Terror squeezed Rachel's heart. It had to be Silly. Something was wrong with Silly. She ran to the phone and dialed Julia's home number.

Seventeen

Both Silly and Julia practically jumped out of their skin when the phone rang, screamingly loud in the silent apartment. Julia looked at Silly for another moment, then went to the phone and picked up the handset on the third ring.

"Hello?"

"Julia! It's Rachel, Silly's mom. Is she okay? I need to talk to her right now!" Rachel was almost in tears, half from panic, and half from relief that at least Julia was okay enough to answer the phone.

Julia hurriedly took the few steps to hand the phone to Silly. "It's your mom," she said.

Silly was still shaking as she raised the phone to her ear. "Mom? What's wrong?" she asked.

"Oh, Silly, I'm so glad you're okay. You're okay, aren't you? I just woke up, and, I don't know, I thought something was terribly wrong, and I had to check on you." Rachel sank to a chair in her own apartment.

"Mom, it's okay, I'm okay. Don't worry. But—I think we need to talk to you. Can you come over?" Silly asked.

Julia gave Silly a curious look, unsure that Rachel would actually believe their story. Silly begged Julia with her eyes, and after a brief pause, Julia nodded in agreement.

"I'll be right there, after I leave Justin a note in case he wakes up," Rachel stood up and hung up the phone.

Julia had returned to the couch next to Silly. "Are you sure you want to tell your mom about this? What is she going to think?"

Silly shook her head. "I don't know what she'll think, but I know I can trust her. My mom will know what to do, and she'd never do anything to hurt us."

The two girls huddled together for warmth and comfort in the now seemingly freezing living room. They didn't speak again until they heard Rachel's knock at the front door.

Julia laughed out loud, in spite of herself. "A knock on the door is what started this whole creepy thing off," she said, as she got up to unlock the door and let Rachel enter.

Rachel barely gave a glance to Julia and ran straight to Silly. "What's wrong? What do you need to talk to me about? You know you can tell me anything. I love you."

"I love you too, Mom. But I don't think I can tell you very much. It's really up to Julia, because I don't remember." Silly had never felt less like her name in her life. Everything felt deathly serious now.

"Julia? What do you mean, Silly, you don't remember? Remember what?" Rachel had briefly calmed down a bit, but the panic was rising again, as was evident by her tone of voice.

Julia and Silly opened their mouths to speak at the same time, looking at each other, but Silly closed hers and nodded at Julia to talk.

"I found a necklace in the couch, Mrs. Sharp, and I didn't know whose it was. Silly didn't know either, and when she touched it, well, she kind of blacked out." Julia knew her voice was shaking, but she didn't know how to control it any better. She hoped she was telling the story the right way, accurately enough to get the truth across, but calmly enough to not scare Silly's mother.

"What do you mean, blacked out?" Rachel looked confused, and stared into Silly's eyes. "You girls aren't—oh, honey, you're not drinking or doing drugs, are you?" The thought seemed inconceivable to Rachel, but it was all she could think of at that moment.

"Of course not, Mom! I hope you know me better than to really think that. It's just, apparently when I took the necklace from Julia, it hypnotized me, or something. I'm not sure exactly what the right word for it is, but when I really looked at the pendant on it, it sent me somewhere else. I don't know how to explain it, because I can't really remember anything but the feelings I had."

"She's telling you the truth, I promise, Mrs. Sharp. She really doesn't know what happened, and all I can tell you is what I saw. She said it was pretty, and she was looking at the spirals, and then she was just staring, this horrible vacant stare. I've never seen anyone look like that, ever. And then she dropped it, and she was okay again, except she didn't remember even seeing the necklace. She tried to pick it back up again, and I stopped her, and I threw it over there," Julia pointed to the side of the room where the necklace had flown.

The three of them looked over where Julia pointed, underneath the front window, but there wasn't a necklace there anymore. There wasn't anything out of place on the carpet. There wasn't a single thing out of place in the room, except the tightly closed bottle of nail polish remover that Silly had knocked over in her haste to get to the popcorn.

The two girls gasped in unison. Rachel turned back and forth from one to the other, confused.

"Are you sure that's what really happened? Are you sure there was a necklace? There has to be a more reasonable explanation than this," Rachel was suspicious. She would never have believed that either girl would lie to her, but still, this was such a crazy, crazy story. How could any of it be true?

Silly and Julia looked at each other, worried. Rachel seemed to be as scared as they were. If Rachel didn't know what to do, how could they figure it out on their own?

Rachel saw the concern in the two girls' faces. These were two of the most honest, responsible teenagers she'd ever heard of. She thought that if they were to make up a story, to start something crazy just for kicks, it would surely have to be something completely off-the-wall like this. Rachel knew they both had active imaginations, and that Silly had been honing hers for almost her entire life. But if this were some kind of trick, then why had she woken up so afraid? She'd known that something was wrong, that something was wrong with Silly. No, it just didn't add up. These girls weren't making up any kind of story; this had to be real. Fear took over Rachel's suspicion, and she took a deep breath and vowed to herself to get to the bottom of this.

"Okay, girls, we're going to find out what's going on. The first thing we have to do is find that necklace. It can't have simply disappeared. We'll find it, and then we'll figure out the next step from there." Rachel had made her decision. This was the truth. They were going to make everything all right again.

The first thing they did was take a deep breath. Then Rachel asked Julia to try to remember exactly where she had been when she'd grabbed the necklace out of Silly's reach. Julia tried to make the same reach and grab that she had only a few minutes before, and pointed in the direction that she was reasonably certain she'd thrown the necklace.

"Silly doesn't need to help look for it, does she? I mean, she can help look, but only with her eyes. She doesn't need to crawl around or feel in the couch. We don't know what could happen to her. That's a good idea, right?" asked Julia.

Silly looked to Rachel for her opinion, and Rachel slowly nodded.

"That's a good point, Julia. Silly, I think it'd be better for you to just walk around the walls and keep an eye on the floor. That way you won't run the risk of accidentally touching the necklace again."

Silly sighed in relief, and got up to begin her first circuit around the room.

"I'll start at the front door and work my way around. That way I'll be almost all the way around before I get to where Julia threw it, so you should probably have found it before then."

Julia headed toward the window, while Rachel began to methodically search the couch, removing all of the cushions and feeling in the cracks on the bottom.

As she knelt down by the spot she was sure the necklace had landed, Julia gasped. Rachel immediately looked up from her own search to make sure that Julia was okay, and that Silly was across the room.

"What is it, Julia?" asked Rachel, warily.

"Th-there's a spot burned into the carpet. It's like something hot was set down for just a second, long enough to leave a mark, but not long enough to burn all the way down through the carpet. I'm pretty sure this is exactly where it hit, but I know it wasn't hot when I touched it, it didn't burn me at all."

Rachel joined Julia by the window, but held a hand up to stop Silly when she began to start that direction.

"Silly, don't come over here just yet. Even if the necklace is somehow gone, leaving just a mark, I don't want you anywhere near it."

Silly saw the wisdom in this, and continued to move farther away from that part of the room. There was a strange feeling building up inside of her, and she didn't like it one bit. It felt almost like she was being pulled toward the burnt spot on the floor, like there were magnets inside her. But there was something else as well. Something dark, and shameful. Silly hadn't ever felt anything like that before. She was too afraid to admit it, even to herself, but it felt like someone else was inside her head, trying to control her body.

Rachel knelt down to examine the spot that Julia had found. It was definitely a burn of some kind, and the shape it formed was like a twisted, broken doll. Rachel knew that a chain can land in any one of a billion different shapes, but this one actually reminded her of Silly. A shiver went down Rachel's spine as she continued to stare at the image burnt into the floor.

There were a body, and two arms, two legs that seemed to be running away. But it was the head and face that absolutely terrified Rachel. The head full of Silly's long hair, blowing behind her, and the face with Silly's nose, the nose she'd gotten from her father. Rachel would know that nose anywhere.

How could so much detail possibly show up in such a tiny space? The entire image was barely larger than a quarter. If the necklace had done this, it must have hit the floor and then piled up almost entirely upon itself. The odds were astronomical of something like that happening, weren't they?

Rachel stopped this line of thinking. She wasn't getting anywhere helpful with it, and besides, this whole situation was completely out of the normal realm of things. Wondering how likely it was that stranger things would continue to happen wouldn't contribute anything to the situation, and could possibly make it worse.

Julia just stared and stared at the spot. From the angle she was looking at, the spot reminded her of something as well. It looked exactly like a Minotaur. Julia had read a story about the fabled beast when she was much younger, and the artist's portrayal had given her nightmares for many, many nights. She hadn't thought about that story in years, but it all came rushing back in an instant. The floodgates of her memory had opened as soon as she recognized what she was seeing. It was like Julia was seven years old again, and afraid of the dark. A tiny whimper escaped from her mouth, and her arm reached up to her face to put her thumb in her mouth as she always had for comfort when she was small.

"Julia? Are you okay?" Rachel put out a hand to steady Julia, who seemed to be leaning, closer and closer to falling over.

Shaking herself, Julia looked up at Rachel. "What does it look like to you?"

Rachel closed her eyes and inhaled deeply through her nose. "It looks like Silly."

Silly's head snapped up from where she had been studying the carpet.

"What? What are you talking about, Mom? What looks like me? I'm coming over there. I don't care what happens." Silly stormed across the room to find out what her mother and friend were watching so intently.

Rachel and Julia both rose, throwing their hands out to stop Silly from coming close enough to see whatever it was that Silly might see. They screamed in unison, "No!!"

Silly stopped, amazed that they were so afraid for her, afraid that they were so afraid, and rapidly becoming afraid for herself.

Rachel put an arm around both girls.

"We're done here. The necklace is nowhere to be found, at least, nowhere it should be found. I think it's best if you two come back home with me for the night. Grab your things, Silly, and Julia, just get something to wear tomorrow. I'll call your parents and let them know that you two won't be staying here alone tonight."

"Are you going to tell them what happened?" asked Julia, concerned most of all that her parents would never let her see Silly again.

"No; at least, not yet. I don't think I could convince anyone of this over the phone. I'll just tell them that you two were scared from all the mischief that's gone on tonight, with kids going door to door knocking, and I insisted that you stay with me for safety's sake. We can talk about what's really going on in more depth tomorrow." Rachel promised Julia.

"Don't worry," Rachel continued, after seeing the concerned looks that both girls shot each other, "I hope you know I would never let anything come between you two. You understand more about friendship than most adults three times your age. Your parents know that too. It will all be okay, I'll make sure of that."

Silly and Julia relaxed a little bit after hearing those words, and Rachel gave them a tiny shove towards Julia's room.

"Come on. I'll check around in here a bit more before we go. Just get your things together."

Neither Silly nor Julia said a word as Silly packed her stuff back into her bag, and Julia shuffled through her closet to find a bag for herself. When Silly was done, she set her bag on Julia's bed and went to the closet to help her friend. Julia turned around with tears in her eyes. Silly wrapped her arms around Julia and the two hugged each other for comfort. After a long moment, they looked into each others eyes, and then continued to pack up Julia's things.

Rachel paced slowly, her eyes tracking back and forth across the floor she was traveling. She forced herself to look everywhere else except that one place. When the temptation to return and grind the image out of the floor became too much to bear, she snatched up a pillow from the couch and gently placed it on the offending spot.

At that moment, the two girls returned from Julia's room, ready to leave. Rachel looked up, guilty, but there were expressions of sympathy and understanding on both young faces. Rachel stood up, and put an arm around each of the girls' shoulders.

"Let's go home," she said.

Leaving the lights on, the three of them walked outside and closed the door firmly behind them. Julia took her keys from her pocket and locked the deadbolt.

With each step away from the apartment that had once been such a treasure trove of happy memories, everyone felt a little lighter, and when they arrived back at Silly's apartment, they all heaved great sighs of relief. Rachel unlocked the front door and quickly ushered the two friends inside, so she could close and relock the door.

Silly thought that once they got home they'd all talk some more about what happened, but she soon realized how sleepy she was. Julia looked exhausted as well, so Rachel gently suggested that they go to bed and talk about it in the morning.

"Everything looks brighter in the sunlight. You two get some rest. I'll call your parents now, Julia. Don't worry. We'll get this squared away," reassured Rachel.

Once in Silly's room, both girls dropped their bags and kicked their shoes off. That was all the preparation for bed they needed, and they curled up in Silly's bed and covered up with the warm blankets. This summer night had definitely become cool.

Rachel picked up her cell phone and dialed Julia's mother, explaining that their daughters had gotten spooked staying home alone and had decided to sleep at Silly's. Julia's mom didn't notice anything wrong with either the story or Rachel's tone of voice until Rachel asked that the two of them come to her apartment when they woke up in the morning.

"Was there some other problem? Are the girls okay?" she asked.

"They're fine, I promise. I think we just need to have a talk with them about staying up late and watching scary movies in the dark," Rachel tried to mask her deeper concerns with some lightheartedness.

"Oh, I know what you mean! I remember seeing some scary movie when I was in college, and I was too scared to leave my dorm room at night for weeks! I guess that's something nobody ever really grows out of. We'll see you tomorrow, then," Julia's mom hung up the phone.

Rachel sat down in her favorite comfy chair in the living room, pulling her feet up underneath her. She wasn't sure that she'd be getting back to sleep that night. It was just too much to take in all at once, though, and Rachel soon drifted to sleep in her chair.

Eighteen

The next morning, Justin was the first person awake, since he'd had an excellent night's sleep, uninterrupted by any kind of paranormal activities. He was mildly surprised to find his mother asleep in the living room, but he knew that sometimes when she missed his dad too much to sleep in a queen size bed she would sit in the living room, looking at old photo albums or just reading until she fell asleep in that room.

He sat down at the kitchen table with a bowl of cereal and thought about what he could do for fun that day. This was actually quite the challenge for Justin, since he usually spent almost his entire summer vacation exploring the neighboring woods with one or several other kids from the apartment complex. He'd never had to really think about what to do with a whole day before this crazy summer had begun. Since the kids had decided on their own that the woods were going to be off limits, none of them could really ask their parents for suggestions, since that would only bring more questioning as to why they had changed their habits so drastically.

He sighed, figuring it would just be another boring summer day, two or three trips to the pool to swim, as long as there weren't too many little kids around, maybe a couple hours of TV, then dinner, then more TV, then bed.

Just then, he heard Rachel stirring in her chair in the living room. Justin slurped the rest of his milk down and put his bowl and spoon in the kitchen sink. He trotted out into the living room to greet his mother, but saw how tired she looked when he got in there, and instead of asking for anything, he simply walked over to her and gave her a big hug.

"I love you, Mom. You look really tired. Why don't you go get in bed and I'll bring you something to eat if you want. How does that sound?" Justin asked.

Rachel smiled at her son. "Thank you for being so thoughtful, Justin. I'd love to get back in bed, but—no, you have an excellent idea there. I will go to bed, but don't make too much noise out here, okay? Silly and Julia came back here to spend the night, and I'm sure they're still sleeping. Would you mind coming to get me if anyone shows up?" she asked.

Justin gave his mom a gigantic smile. "Thanks for noticing that I can take care of myself just fine! I'll be quiet. Why did they come back here? I thought they had big plans for Julia's birthday and all that."

"They just got scared being home alone and needed a grownup around. I know you think you're grown, but everybody gets scared sometimes. Thanks for taking care of things for me this morning so I can get a bit more rest." Rachel really appreciated Justin's gesture, and hugged him again after she stood up and stretched.

"I'll be up in a couple of hours or so. Goodnight!"

"Goodnight, Mom!" replied Justin.

So, the girls got scared, huh? Justin thought to himself. What a couple of weenies! He stopped himself. Maybe he shouldn't really make fun of anybody else. After all, he and his friends were pretty scared to go back and play in the woods anymore. Yeah, it was probably best to keep the name-calling down to a minimum, at least until they could take the woods back as their playground.

With that issue resolved, Justin grabbed a book off the shelf and settled himself into the couch cushions for a nice read. That was something quiet he could do, and stay around the house to find out if anything really scary had happened to his sister and her best friend the night before.

Nineteen

There was a lot more to the reason behind Justin and the other kids' decision to stay out of the woods from now on than he had let on to his sister. It wasn't just 'bad feelings' that had caused them all to beware.

About a week before school let out for the summer, one of the other kids from the apartment complex had gone into the woods and spent the night there. He wasn't someone Justin knew well, or even at all other than to recognize his face on the school bus. After that night, though, every kid knew his name was Scott.

One Friday night, Scott had decided that the stories he'd heard about strange noises in the woods needed to be investigated. He asked just about everyone he knew to join him in camping out for the night, but no one was willing to do it. There had grown to be just way too many rumors about what was living in the woods. Some kids claimed it was a bear, others a mountain lion, some said ghosts, a few voted for Bigfoot, and one or two were absolutely certain that it was some kind of man-eating monster.

Scott wasn't particularly big, strong, or brave, but he wanted to find out and put the rumors to rest, once and for all. When he was unable to find any witnesses to camp with him, he didn't back out. Scott had too much pride for that. He just decided to bring an extra camera to record what he saw or heard out there in the middle of the night.

Four kids did help him bring everything out to his campsite, as close to the middle of the woods as they could guess. Scott set up a tent, and brought food and water, along with a sleeping bag and two video cameras. The four kids with him watched him set up one of the cameras in a nearby tree, facing the front of his tent, so he could record all of his own coming and going that night. The other camera Scott decided to keep constantly at his side. If something happened, he didn't want to have to run away and leave both cameras behind to be possibly stolen or destroyed. He wanted at least one to carry with him.

After everything was set up, the other kids went home. It was nearly dark, and they were definitely ready to get out of the woods for the night, if not forever. Scott began to gather up some sticks to start a small fire. He'd been a scout for years, so he was sure that he could safely build a fire that wouldn't spread and cause damage to the woods.

Once the fire had begun crackling in the small pit that Scott had dug, he sat down near it with his pack to review his supplies. He had made sure that he had plenty of batteries for his flashlight, and that both cameras were fully charged. The six gallon jugs of water he'd brought were lined up along one inside wall of his tent, and his snacks were all sealed in plastic bags to keep the smell as unobtrusive as possible.

Scott didn't plan on using his flashlight very much, because he wanted to be able to keep his night vision. He faced away from the fire as long as it was bright and sat and waited to see what would happen.

As he waited, his mind wandered to all the different explanations he might be able to discover for the noises that had been heard in the woods lately. Normal forest creatures and wind were the most likely explanation, he told himself. And he believed that, mostly. Still, there was a small part of Scott that was secretly terribly afraid of what would happen to him. He knew the woods were way too small for even a single bear or mountain lion, but what if there really were such things as ghosts? If there wasn't enough room for a bear or lion, Bigfoot wouldn't be able to survive either, but what if he was just passing through?

The story that scared Scott the most of all, however, was one he'd overheard at school one afternoon. There had been some kids talking at the next table in the cafeteria, kids that Scott knew had never even been to these woods, but the entire school knew what the gossip was. This group in particular had a pretty good handle on what kinds of noises people were hearing, even if they did believe that kids had been turning up missing. Of course no one was missing, if they were, that would be even bigger news at school.

But the part that had really struck Scott was their theory of what was living in the woods and causing all of this commotion. One of the kids had suggested that it was the essence of pure evil. He said that there used to real monsters roaming the earth, and that one of them had set up shop here. When it had killed and eaten every living thing in the area, it had gone to sleep in the middle of those woods, a sort of hibernation that had lasted thousands of years. Maybe it had finally woken back up, or maybe it was just having some dreams about waking up, but he was pretty sure of himself as he told his friends about this theory.

Scott told himself he didn't believe the story. Monsters were just fairy tales, after all. But now, sitting in the woods in the dark, all by himself except for his campfire and his two cameras, Scott was beginning to have his doubts.

He decided to have a snack to keep his mind off darker things while he settled in for the night. He'd only started a small fire, and it wouldn't last long. He used the last of its light to pick the good bits out of the bag of trail mix he'd brought, and took a large swig from his first jug of water.

Scott paused to listen carefully to the surrounding woods. As he sat in the stillness, he soon realized that things seemed a little too still. The chirping birds and scampering squirrels that he'd heard during the daylight hours didn't seem to be nesting anywhere nearby. There wasn't even any breeze to stir the leaves in the treetops above him. A chill ran up Scott's spine, and he shivered.

"Okay, just snap out of this!" he told himself aloud, more to dispel the silence, if only for a moment, than to truly reassure himself.

The tactic did not pay off; if anything, the woods seemed even quieter now than they had before he'd spoken. Scott was starting to think that maybe this trip had not been his best idea.

He took his trail mix and gallon of water and retreated into the tent to lie down. A rest before it got really late could be just the thing to help him feel a little better about this whole situation that he'd gotten himself into. Scott stretched out on his sleeping bag and stared up at the dark ceiling of the tent. The trees in this spot were so thick that not enough moonlight made it down far enough to shine through the weave of the tent fabric above him. He glanced through the open entrance to see the blinking red light on the camera he'd affixed to the tree, proving that it was still faithfully recording.

Just then, he thought he saw a shadow flit by behind his campfire. He turned his head, but it was already gone, if anything had been there in the first place. Scott blinked a few times to make sure he wasn't simply blinded by the dwindling light from his fire, but no. His eyes were fine. It was the woods themselves that weren't okay.

Scott lay back down and closed his eyes, trying to empty his mind and not think about anything, just focus on what he could hear, what he could sense in the woods outside. Suddenly his eyes snapped back open and he sat bolt upright. There was some strange shuffling sound right outside the tent!

He was too afraid to move; he might scare whatever it was away, or draw its attention, and he didn't want either of those outcomes. He could hear his heartbeat thudding in his ears, much louder than anything outside. He took deep breaths and tried to calm himself down. This was the whole reason he'd done this in the first place, to find out if anything would happen! He couldn't possibly chicken out now.

As he kept his breathing slow and steady, he tried to turn his head a bit to see if that would help make the sounds any clearer for

Scott collapsed onto the couch, and his mother sat down next to him. She could see that he was frightened, and it scared her. She'd never seen him like this before.

"Did someone put you up to this? I'll just bet they did, and had someone waiting to scare you out there. Is that what happened? Please tell me," she begged.

Scott looked his mother in the eyes.

"No, Mom, I volunteered to do it. There've been a lot of kids scared in the woods lately, saying they heard some weird sounds, but I didn't believe them. I should have," Scott told her.

"I'm sorry I left all my stuff out there, but the other kids who helped me set up will get it for me tomorrow, I promise. I don't know if I will be able to help them, but I'll try, Mom. I'll try," Scott tried to put a brave face on, but he knew he wasn't succeeding very well.

"Honey, it's okay. You learned your lesson, didn't you? And you won't ever do anything like this again, right? What's done is done, and I'm just glad you're safe and sound," replied his mother.

"Thanks, Mom. I really appreciate that. I think, if it's okay with you, that I'd just really like to go to bed. I'm so tired now that I'm home again, and all I want is to rest," Scott said.

"Of course you can. And if any kids come knocking on the door in the morning, I won't let on that I know anything about this. I know how kids can be," vowed his mother.

"Good night, Mom. I love you," said Scott.

"I love you, too, good night," replied his mother.

After Scott went to bed, his mother promptly forgot that Scott said he'd volunteered, and blamed the whole incident on some bad influences from school. She loved her son, but sometimes she didn't quite pay enough attention to what he said.

When Scott woke up the next morning, after a deep, restful sleep that came from the knowledge that nothing could get him in his own bed, he got up and got dressed. First things first, he thought, as he checked the camera he'd brought home with him.

As he reviewed the video, at first it seemed as though he hadn't caught a thing, but after watching four times, Scott caught a glimpse of something new. His arm had been down when the noise had come back, but he'd swung it up to run at just the right instant, catching a few frames of a large pair of glowing red eyes.

Scott froze the video on the scene with those eyes. He stared into them until he was barely breathing. With a great effort, he tore himself away from the screen and turned the monitor off.

Scott leaned back in his chair and thought about what he should do. After this, there was no way he'd ever go back into those woods, and his conscience wouldn't let him send anyone else to retrieve his things without a full disclosure of what had happened to him the night before. He knew he had to tell the other kids about this, or someone was going to get hurt. He made his mind up, and started to get dressed.

Camera in hand, Scott called to his mother that he was going outside to hang out with some friends. She acknowledged him from the kitchen, where she was putting groceries away from her early morning shopping trip. Scott headed out the front door with a firm step.

Scott's first stop was his best friend Roger's house. He knocked on the door and politely asked if Roger could come out. Roger came tearing around the corner, anxious to hear what had happened to Scott the previous night.

"Let's go," said Scott. "We need to get everyone together right now."

"But what happened?" Roger wanted to know, and right now!

"Bad things. We need to make sure everyone knows, and nobody ever goes back there," Scott said.

The two split up and began canvassing the apartment complex, getting all the kids to help them gather everyone in the parking lot next to the woods.

When everyone that they could find was together, Roger waved everyone quiet so that Scott could speak.

"You all know I was staying in the woods last night to find out what's really going on. I'll start by telling you that I didn't stay all night. I had to escape and run for my life, but I caught some video of what was chasing me right here." Scott held his camera up so they could all see.

"Everyone needs to see this, but we're going to have to take turns, so please, be patient. We have all day to watch, and there's not much to see, but there's enough."

The kids closest to Scott grouped around him to watch the video. At first they were nonplussed, but when Scott paused the playback at the right moment to capture the eyes, they gasped.

It took over an hour, but by then, everyone there had watched the video and was thoroughly convinced that Scott was telling the truth, that there really was something out there haunting those woods. That they should stay away, at all costs.

Even so, a few kids maintained that it was a good idea to go out to Scott's campsite and collect his things, especially the other camera. Maybe it had gotten better footage of whatever that thing was. Scott vehemently defended his position that it was a bad idea, that they should just chalk up his things as a loss, but after a long argument, seven kids agreed that they would go back in the woods, one last time.

Everyone gathered at the edge of the woods to see them off, and then waited, holding their breath, hoping against hope that they would all make it back safe and sound, since it was daytime.

In less than twenty minutes, all seven came back out of the woods, each carrying some portion of Scott's equipment and supplies. The first one out, Steven, had Scott's camera, and he handed it over, out of breath.

"Everything looked fine, like nobody had messed with it. I don't think the thing cared about your stuff after you got away," Steven told Scott.

"Thank you guys, all of you, so much for doing this. I couldn't ask you, but I really appreciate it. Let's see if this camera can tell us anything else," replied Scott.

The other six dropped their loads of supplies and gathered around Scott as he fast forwarded through the images of himself sitting by his fire. He slowed down to normal speed once he got to the part when he retired into his tent, remembering that was the first time he'd heard the noises.

As Scott related what had happened to him the night before, they watched the playback. There were the sounds Scott had heard, clear as day, but absolutely no detectable motion anywhere within the camera's field of vision.

Suddenly, Steven pointed and shouted out, "There!"

Scott hurriedly paused the video, and sure enough, the same

glowing red eyes menacingly stared down the camera lens. The kids looked at each other, growing more frightened by the minute.

Scott decided to skip ahead to the time he decided to leave. He began playing the video again when he saw himself exiting his tent, camera in one hand, gallon of water in the other. They watched as he approached this camera, and then--nothing. The images dissolved into staticky snow on the screen. Scott groaned, and tried to skip past the bad part, but when the interference finally stopped, Scott was already gone, along with whatever monster it was that had chased him out of the woods.

By the time the second camera had been passed around and everyone had seen the new footage, or lack thereof, it was time for many of the kids to be home for lunch. Before they all scattered to their separate homes, they all agreed to never go into the woods again, and also to not get any parents involved, because this was just too crazy for adults to believe.

This was a promise they all knew they would keep.

Twenty

Around eleven that morning, Justin heard someone knocking on the front door. He closed his book, the second of that day so far, and went to answer it. Without checking the peephole, he opened the door to find Julia's parents on the welcome mat.

"Hi, Justin, is your mom busy? And are the girls up yet? I'll be they stayed up all night gossiping," smiled Julia's mom.

"Oh yeah, they're all asleep. I'll go get my mom for you, though. She might be awake in her room anyway. Hold on. Oops, I mean, come in and have a seat. Sorry! I try not to forget my manners too often," Justin said.

Julia's parents came in and sat on the couch together while Justin ran off to Rachel's room to see if she was up yet. When he raised his hand to knock on her door, he heard stirring, so he knocked gently and waited for his mom to invite him in.

"Good morning, Justin. Thanks again for letting me sleep. What's up?" asked Rachel.

"Julia's parents are here, and they wanted to talk to you about something," answered Justin.

"Oh, I forgot all about that! Let me throw on some fresh clothes, and I'll be right out. See if they want something to drink, would you, sweetie?" Rachel gave Justin a quick hug before disappearing into her closet.

"Sure, Mom!" said Justin, and he went back to the living room.

"She'll be out in a just a minute. Do you guys want anything to drink?" he asked.

They both asked for water, and Justin trotted into the kitchen to grab two glasses. He came back out with the ice water and set it on the coffee table in front of them just as Rachel came out of the hallway.

"I'm so sorry, I forgot I asked you two to come by. I feel like I was up half the night calming those girls down!" said Rachel, as she sat down on one of the living room chairs.

Justin knew what he was supposed to do, so he grabbed his book up and sauntered down the hallway to his room. He'd have loved to eavesdrop, but he knew his mom would tell him what was going on as soon as her visitors left anyway, so he didn't worry about it.

"What happened last night, Rachel?" asked Julia's mom, while her husband was taking a big gulp of water.

"Well, I woke up and had this feeling that something wasn't right. You know, that maternal instinct annoyance? Justin was fine so I called to check on the girls. When Julia answered she sounded so afraid, so I got dressed and ran down there to check on them," Rachel paused for a second in her tale, noticing the lack of interest on both of Julia's parents' faces. That wasn't like them at all; this was a couple that took a hugely active interest in their daughter's life, not to mention Silly's life as well, since she was Julia's best friend. One was looking out the window while the other studied the condensation on the outside of his water glass. That feeling that Rachel had felt last night came back in full force. Something was wrong; she shouldn't be telling Julia's parents what really happened last night.

"Those two were watching some kind of scary movie, and when some other kids starting going door to door knocking, it really just scared the crap out of them. You know that uneasy feeling when you're home alone and you hear a knock, but no one's there? That's all it really was. But they were still scared, so I invited them to come back home, and here we are!" finished Rachel, petering out at the end of her story.

"I thought that was all. But why would you want to talk to us about that?" asked Julia's mom. "That's no big deal, nothing to have a conference about."

Rachel stuttered a moment before finding her bearings again. "Well, I just—I just wanted you to know, in case they left a mess or something. They were behaving; it was some other kids who were misbehaving. I'll find out who it was and make sure their parents give them a good talking-to. Just trying to keep you in the loop, is all, really."

"Well, all right, I just don't see why we needed to have a face-to-face for that. I was content with what you told me on the phone last night. But as they say, no harm, no foul, am I right?" Julia's mom laughed quietly to herself, set her glass back on the coffee table, and stood up. Julia's father stood up with her, and without having said a word the entire time he was in Rachel's apartment, opened the front door and left.

Rachel relaxed into her chair, and made a face as she wondered what could possibly be going on with Julia's parents. They'd always, always been interested in Julia and Silly's escapades before, and the silence on Julia's dad's part was particularly uncharacteristic. Still, no one ever knows the whole story when it's someone else's story, Rachel told herself. She'd just have to let it go and make sure she was keeping a good eye on the girls for a while, until whatever was going on with Julia's parents resolved itself.

"Justin! You can come back out now!" Rachel called.

Justin promptly opened his door and returned to the living room, where he curled back up on the couch, although he left his book closed for the moment.

"What was that about?" he asked.

"Nothing, really," replied Rachel. "I shouldn't have asked them to come by. I guess something important is going on in their lives right now. Oh well," she finished.

Justin's disappointment in the lack of gossip was clearly evident in his posture and facial expression.

"How about you get those lazy bums out of bed and we have some serious breakfast?" Rachel suggested.

Justin grinned, and immediately hopped off the couch, his book falling to the floor.

"Sounds great, Mom! But I hate to tell you this, it's lunchtime already," he smiled mischievously at Rachel as he scampered out of the room and down the hallway.

"That child!" sighed Rachel, grinning to herself as she headed into the kitchen to see what she could fix for a lunch for four.

Justin pounded with both fists on Silly's door, trying to scare both girls awake. He loved his sister and her best friend Julia, but he loved even more to cause some trouble every now and then!

When he could hear moaning and groaning through the door, he paused to see if he would need to run. When no one threw the door open to chase him away, he decided to continue the fun.

"Wake up, wake up, wake up! You're late for school!" Justin groaned to himself. Couldn't he come up with anything better than that? For crying out loud, that was the lamest excuse for annoying he'd ever thought of. At least he'd woken them up; he shrugged, and left to go see what his mom was doing in the kitchen.

Silly and Julia were still completely exhausted. Their adventure of the night before had taken so much more out of both of them than they were willing to admit. Silly had had the same bad dreams for most of the night, and Julia's were haunted by the Minotaur from her childhood.

The daylight soon brought some comfort to the pair, however, and they tried to shake off as much weariness as they could before getting up and dressed. Julia quickly realized she was trying to put on a shirt as a pair of shorts, and her laughter was infectious enough to disperse the rest of the blues from the room.

With a bounce in her step, Silly exited her room and went down the hall to the bathroom. Julia finished gathering her things back together and waited impatiently for her turn. When Silly was done, she came out and gave Julia a smile on her way to the kitchen.

Rachel had laid out a smorgasbord of sandwich fixings, from bread to meat to veggies and spreads. Silly piped a cheerful good morning to her brother and mom and headed to the refrigerator for some orange juice.

"About time you sleepyheads got out of bed!" chided Rachel, who wasn't about to share the secret that she'd slept nearly as long as the teenagers. She softened her reproof with a smile to her daughter.

Justin was nearly finished layering a sandwich that had to be too tall for his mouth. Silly shook her head at his eating habits. As Julia joined them, Rachel began her much more sensibly sized turkey and cheddar on wheat, and Silly took two plates and handed one to Julia.

"Looks like it's sandwiches for breakfast, is that cool with you?" Silly asked her friend.

"I feel like I haven't eaten in a week! Sandwiches sound great to me," smiled Julia.

Justin pulled a bag of chips from the top of the refrigerator and sat down at the dinner table with his plate, the chips, and a glass of juice. Rachel joined him while the girls finished making their own sandwiches.

"Thanks for not letting them know about my hypocrisy," she whispered to Justin. "You know they'd love making fun of me for sleeping half the day!"

Justin smiled conspiratorially back at her, a mouthful of sandwich making it impossible for him to reply just then.

Silly and Julia came out of the kitchen together and sat down at the table.

"Thanks for coming over last night," said Julia.

"Yeah, Mom, thank you," agreed Silly.

"Oh, it's no problem, girls. I love you and just want you two to be happy and safe," replied Rachel.

"Your parents came by this morning," said Rachel. "I let them know that the two of you were just freaked out by a movie and those kids knocking on doors. They weren't worried, but I just wanted to let them know."

Silly and Julia took this as an understanding that Julia's parents wouldn't find out anything about the necklace, or anything else that had happened the night before, until further notice. Julia was visibly relieved, as her main concern had been that when her parents found out, they wouldn't let her associate with Silly anymore. Silly hadn't been sure if her mother would tell them or not, but she realized that she was very relieved herself that it was still a secret between the three of them.

After a glance at Justin to make sure he didn't understand what she was talking about, Rachel continued. "Since that was the only thing that scared you last night, I didn't think I needed to wake you up to go home, Julia. And your parents didn't say anything about you having to come home at a specific time, so you're welcome to hang out here all day if you want to do that."

"Thank you, Mrs. Sharp; I think I'd like that. I know Silly and I have some things to talk about. Just girl talk, you know," said Julia. She wasn't quite sure whether or not Justin knew anything else, but she wanted to make sure without revealing anything.

Silly had caught the glance, and knew that her mom hadn't said anything to Justin, so she went along with Julia's story. "You know how we girls like to talk!" she smiled.

"I've got to open the office up when I finish eating, or I'll be behind for the next week, but if you need anything, you can always come by and ask. There's nothing that I can't interrupt for a bit if you need some advice." Rachel wanted to be sure that the girls knew she was there for them. What had happened the night before had absolutely terrified her, and she envied the way these two teenagers seemed to bounce back like nothing had happened.

"In case you forgot, I'm still here!" Justin piped up. "I'm not too dumb to realize that you guys are talking about something you don't want me to know about. I just hope it's something dumb like boys or periods. I do know you talk about those things."

The girls laughed, and then Rachel joined in. It was great to be able to laugh without fear.

Twenty-One

Life seemed for a brief moment to get back to normal for Silly, but the normalcy was like an Indian summer in that it escaped again so quickly.

Silly and Julia believed that they had exhausted every possible explanation for the incident with the necklace. They'd had meetings with Rachel several times to discuss it, and many more meetings between the two of them.

Julia desperately wanted to maintain that the whole episode was a mass hallucination, that the crazy combination of the beauty products she and Silly had used on Julia's birthday had resulted in some kind of drug that made them dream the whole thing up.

Silly knew that while she would love to delude herself as Julia seemed to be doing, there was no way that Julia's explanation could be real. There was the spot on the carpet, for one thing, which Julia explained away as a spill. But there was something else for Silly. In her calmer dreams, she knew that the necklace was real, and she tried and tried to find out its true meaning during her waking hours.

The bad dreams had continued to worsen for Silly. Night after night, her mother checked on her when the screams became too much to bear. Night after night, the same story. Silly always told her mother that she didn't have any idea why she was screaming. It wasn't that Silly didn't remember the dreams; it was that she didn't want to.

Silly preferred to discuss her other dreams, the ones about the necklace. There was one in particular that came almost every night, as soon as she put her head to her pillow.

It was the living room all over again, but this time Silly remembered what happened after she touched the necklace. As soon as the gold made contact with her fingers, Silly felt herself moving back and away from Julia's couch and living room. Faster and faster she sped backwards, until she could barely make Julia's concerned face out at the other end of a dark, shadowy tunnel, like looking up from the bottom of the deepest well.

Suddenly Silly would hear a sound, like a shuffling, sliding step. She turned her head sharply to the left, but she was still surrounded by darkness. The only light was that which somehow sank down from the other end of the tunnel to pool directly around where Silly sat. Nothing outside that small circle was visible, at least, not to Silly.

Still, she had this feeling that she was surrounded by someone or something, maybe some kind of creature that lived in this hole. The shuffling sound came closer and closer, until Silly knew that whatever was the source must be near enough to reach out and touch her. But just then, Silly snapped back to Julia's living room, because she'd dropped the necklace.

Silly didn't know how to stay in that dream long enough to find out what was surrounding her. She wished more than anything that she could have one more minute, one more second of time there. Whatever it was frightened her, but she was so much more afraid of never finding out what was going on. She just had to find a way to stay in that dream, to make contact with those creatures.

Night after night, she never did. The dream stayed the same; her questions remained unanswered.

But there were the other dreams. Those continued to develop, continued to worsen. These were the dreams that had Silly waking up screaming, drenched in sweat, out of breath as though she'd been running for miles and miles.

Those were the dreams that Silly and Rachel both feared. All Rachel wanted was for her daughter to be okay, to be able to get one single night of undisturbed sleep. To escape these demons that haunted her. But Silly couldn't, and Rachel didn't know what she could do to help.

Finally, Silly agreed to tell Rachel what she could remember of these dreams. It was a lot harder for Silly to talk about these; they were so much harder to remember than the simple ones about the necklace. But she said she was willing to try.

They were always almost the same, but always a little bit different. Sometimes it was the scenery that changed the slightest bit; sometimes Silly's clothes were different. Somehow she knew that there were also variances in the time that the dream was taking place, although it was always in the dead of night.

It always started with a forest, and Silly ran and ran with something horrible chasing her. She didn't know where she had started running, or why what it was chased her; the dream always started after that. She ran through the trees, with branches snagging her clothing and roots catching her feet, making her stumble. Sometimes she fell, sometimes she regained her balance. No matter what happened, she knew she had to keep going.

That used to be all that Silly could ever remember, but now, she could remember how close her pursuer was getting. She could remember feeling its hot breath on the back of her neck. She could remember the terribly dry rawness in her throat from screaming.

But she never turned around; she never saw what was following her. She couldn't waste the time to turn her head and possibly trip and fall, letting it catch her. Oh, how she wanted to. She wanted to give up and let it do whatever it was trying to do. Maybe then the dreams would stop. Maybe then she could get some rest.

This was all that she told Rachel. Even when they continued to worsen, again and again, she never let on to her mother that anything had changed.

Rachel knew, of course. She could see how this was taking its toll on Silly. Rachel could see the dark circles under Silly's eyes getting darker, and she could see how the clothes that used to fit began to hang from Silly's already small frame. But she didn't know what else to do for Silly. After one terrible night of over the counter sleep medication, when Silly screamed all night long without being able to wake up, Rachel was afraid to try anything else. Silly refused to see her doctor because she was afraid that he would tell her she was crazy and lock her up. All Rachel could do anymore was pray.

And still the dreams became worse. Silly began to remember more and more of them in her waking hours, which she tried to stretch out as long as possible, so she could avoid dreaming. Trying to stay awake didn't mean that she could stay awake, however. Silly learned that if she didn't keep to her usual bedtime, she would fall asleep wherever she was, and sleepwalk to her bed, to dream.

The first time that happened, Silly assumed that Rachel and Justin had put her back in her own bed when they found her on the couch. She didn't say anything about it, but the next night, when the same thing happened again, she did ask, and learned that neither her mother nor her brother knew anything about it. The third night, Silly began dreaming as she was on her way to her bed, and Rachel got up again when she heard the screaming. Rachel couldn't even turn Silly away from her bedroom, let alone wake her up. The next morning, when they talked about it, Silly agreed to give in to this one request from Rachel, and go to bed when she needed to go to bed. At least that way, Rachel wouldn't have to worry about Silly falling over anything as she was sleepwalking.

It had now been three weeks since the incident with the necklace, and Silly, Rachel and Julia were all nearly at their wits' end. Silly had nearly given up all hope of a normal life, and Julia's sleep was beginning to be affected by her worry over her best friend's situation. Rachel had actually stopped checking on Silly at night, and just let her be. There was nothing Rachel could do for Silly while she was asleep anyway.

One evening, the three of them decided to have one last meeting about Silly. They agreed to meet in Rachel's office the next morning so that Justin couldn't possibly overhear, since he still didn't know what was going on. Justin was the only person Rachel had ever heard of who could sleep through everything that he'd been sleeping through for nearly a month.

Of course, the next morning, Silly woke after another grueling night of dreams. Rachel woke worried about Silly, as did Julia. The three of them got dressed and ready in their apartments, and then met in the front office to decide what their remaining options were.

They all sat down, and Rachel and Julia shared a glance before Rachel took a deep breath and turned to Silly.

"Silly, it's time. It's time you see a doctor. Don't forget that you are not legally responsible for yourself yet, and that if something were to happen to you, I could lose both you and Justin, forever. I don't want that to happen. I'm not going to be accused of neglecting my only daughter. I'm making you an appointment," Rachel stated.

Julia nodded in agreement with Rachel. The two of them had agreed upon this course of action before attempting to set up this meeting with Silly, without Silly's knowledge. Silly looked from one to the other, unbelieving. Then reality sank in, and the shock turned to anger. Silly was furious.

"How dare you do this to me? You know what he'll say. You know what any doctor will say. I'm crazy, that's all. They'll dope me up and keep me in restraints so I can drool on myself for the rest of my life. NO!! There has to be some other way. There has to be some other solution. I can't believe you would do this! My best friend and my mother, trying to get rid of me! I'm not going. I'm just not. I don't care what you say. I hate you both!" Silly ran from the office, and didn't stop until she was safe in her own room, where she pushed her dresser against the door so no one would be able to come in.

As soon as Silly left the room, Rachel sobbed, and put her head in her hands. Julia got up and went behind Rachel's desk to put her arm around her best friend's grieving mother. Rachel only sobbed harder at the comforting touch.

"I just don't know what to do anymore, Julia. I don't know what to do with Silly; I don't know what to do with myself. I don't understand why any of this is happening. What did any of us do to deserve this? All I want is to go back to the way things were. Things were fine. Things were perfect. I guess I just didn't appreciate it enough," Rachel trailed off, and began crying in earnest. Julia hugged her harder, and tried to reassure her.

"Don't worry. She'll be okay. She'll realize that we're right, that she has to get some help. If she doesn't get some real sleep, she'll never be able to function. She won't be able to go back to the way she was. And you know as well as I do it's not your fault at all. It's nobody's fault. This is some crazy thing that happened and nobody understands it, but something will happen to make it all okay. Something will make it right. I just know it," said Julia.

Julia's speech full of hope seemed to do what for Rachel what her embrace could not. Rachel took a deep, ragged breath, wiped her face, and looked Julia in the eyes.

"You're right, Julia. Something is going to make it right. I don't know how you know that, and I don't know how I know that, but it's true. I feel it too," Rachel agreed.

It was true; both Rachel and Julia felt something different today. It was almost like waking up for the first day of school, that excitement in the pit of your stomach that swims among the dread of going back to school, that little hope that this year things will be great, that yearning to meet new people and make new friends.

Finally, they recognized that feeling. It was hope. Hope that had been gone from their lives for too long, but had finally come back to its rightful place.

Twenty-Two

Silly waited in her room for hours, it seemed. When she had finished shuffling her furniture around to prevent unauthorized entry, she threw herself on her bed, where she scooted all the way back to the corner and sat with her back to the wall. She drew her knees up to her chest and wrapped her arms around them before dropping her head to rest her forehead on her knees.

She was so tired, but she knew that there was no chance at all that she'd be able to go to sleep, even if she tried. Some outside force was completely in control of her sleep patterns now. Silly hated that feeling of not being herself, of not being in control. All she wanted was one day of her old life back, but that's the one thing that she feared she might never have.

As she closed her eyes, Silly tried desperately to remember everything from her dreams. She wanted to find the missing piece, the one clue that would tie everything together and somehow make it all make sense again.

The dream about the necklace hadn't changed, had it? She went away, and she waited at the end of that long, dark tunnel. What about the sounds? Was there anything at all familiar about them?

This was the same line of searching that Silly had gone over and over countless times before, but this time, something was different. There was something familiar about those sounds. They almost sounded like—Silly squeezed herself tighter into a ball, trying to squeeze the answer from her memory.

Under the shuffling, sliding feet, very faintly, so faintly that she had never noticed before, something familiar. A voice calling to her, telling her to stay calm, telling her that she wasn't alone. Whose voice was it?

Silly lifted her head and stared at the wall in front of her. She did know that voice. It was Chase. She had to find Chase and make sure that it really was his voice that she was hearing. She had to know if it was him reassuring her.

Silly stretched out her cramped arms and legs and rose from her bed. She began pulling on her dresser, trying to get it far enough away from the door to allow it to open again. She was so tired, and without adrenaline to help her anymore, it was close to impossible for her to move the heavy furniture. Somehow she managed to slide it out of the way, after long minutes of tugging. She opened her door and poked her head out into the hallway.

Why weren't Julia and Rachel out there waiting for her to give up and come out? Silly wondered. Justin wasn't even around. When she took a few steps down the hall, however, she heard voices coming from the dining room. Silly slowly walked into the dining room, and all three of the people she'd wondered about were sitting at the table, having lunch.

As soon as Silly stepped into the room, they all looked up at her. Rachel stood up, and went to Silly, arms open to hug her daughter. Silly stepped into them and hugged her mother as though she hadn't seen her for years. Silly closed her eyes and knew that everything would be okay.

Julia and Justin got up from the table as well, and joined the group hug. All Justin knew was that something was wrong with Silly, but he was determined that he'd figure the rest out on his own before anyone decided to fill him in. Julia was simply happy that Silly had come out of her room on her own.

Silly opened her mouth, about to tell them about Chase's voice, but for some reason she decided to keep that to herself, for now. She wouldn't be going back to sleep for hours yet, so she had all day to find him and make sure that it really was his voice that she'd been hearing.

With her arm still around Silly's shoulders, Rachel escorted her to her chair at the dinner table.

"Would you like something to drink, Silly?" Rachel asked.

Silly nodded her head, relieved that there didn't seem to be any more push to send her to the doctor, at least, not right at this moment. She sat down and accepted the orange juice that Rachel brought her with a small thanks.

"I think I'll have lunch and then just watch some TV, if that's okay with you, Mom. I'm sorry, Julia, but I'd really like some time to myself to pretend that everything is all right again, even if it's just for an afternoon," Silly said.

Julia nodded. "That's okay with me, Silly. I'll just go home and hang around the house today. I'm sure my parents think I've just about disowned them recently, with all the time I've been spending over here. You can call me later, if you want to, or wait until tomorrow. I'll just leave you be, for now."

Julia had already finished eating, so she thanked Rachel for lunch and smiled at Silly and Justin·before leaving.

"I need to get back to the office," said Rachel. "Are you kids going to be okay here for the afternoon?"

Silly looked up at her mother.

"We'll be fine, Mom. I'll take care of Silly if she needs anything," answered Justin.

"Thanks, Justin," said Silly and Rachel, at the same time.

Rachel got up and hugged her kids one more time before heading back to work. "I'll be home in a few hours, there's nothing that desperately needs doing, but you know I'm getting behind. I love you two." And she left.

Justin stood up and began gathering up their plates.

"Can I fix you anything to eat, Silly?" he asked.

Silly shook her head, finished her juice, and got up to go into the living room, where she sat on the couch without turning the television on. She leaned back into the cushions and closed her eyes for a minute.

By the time Justin finished cleaning up and made it into the living room, Silly was fast asleep, the first peaceful sleep she'd had in weeks. Justin covered her with a blanket and went to his room so as not to disturb her.

Silly slept and slept. Justin remained in his room, but he had left his door open in case Silly needed anything. He lay in his bed and read his favorite book. He wasn't really bothered by having to stay inside; since none of the kids were exploring the woods anymore, he didn't seem to have much interest in any other pastimes.

Twenty-Three

That night, while Silly and her family were sitting down to dinner, there was a knock at their front door. Rachel rolled her eyes and walked into the living room to answer. She was momentarily taken aback when she checked the peephole, but went ahead and opened the door to let Chase in.

"Hi, Chase, what can I do for you?" Rachel asked.

"I'd like to talk to Silly, if that's okay with you, ma'am. I'm sorry to come at dinnertime, I didn't realize you'd be eating so early," he apologized.

"It's okay, it's just been a long day, so we were all planning to call it a day and turn in early. I'll go get Silly. Why don't you have a seat on the couch?" Rachel stepped back and pointed Chase in the right direction, then returned to the dining room for Silly.

"Who was it, Mom?" asked Justin.

"It's Chase, for Silly," Rachel replied, nodding at Silly. "He's waiting for you in the living room. I didn't know you two were friends. He's never come by or called before, has he? Never mind, I'll find out later. Why don't you go see what's going on and then come back to dinner? Our curiosity can wait," Rachel finished, with a glare for Justin to keep his mouth shut.

Silly frowned a bit. "No, we're not friends. We ride the bus together and had biology, but that's it. I'll be right back."

Silly stood up and straightened her shirt and brushed some stray hairs back from her face. Chase or not, a boy in her living room was a boy in her living room, and she had to at least try to look presentable, even if she hadn't left the apartment all day.

When Silly came in, Chase stood up to greet her.

"Hi, Silly. I know we haven't really talked to each other much since I moved here, but there are some important things we need to talk about now, some things that have been going on that I probably know a lot more about than you do. Do you have any idea what I'm talking about?" Chase waited expectantly for Silly to answer or simply sit down.

Silly's jaw dropped, but then she quickly realized that Chase couldn't possibly be talking about what she was thinking. He couldn't know anything about the necklace or her dreams, could he? She sat down on the opposite end of the couch from where Chase was standing.

"No, I don't think I do know what you're talking about. What is it? If it's something about your apartment, I'm sure my mom would be the person to talk to. You know she's the manager, right?" Silly asked.

"It's not about any apartment at all. And I have a feeling that you know exactly what's been going on lately. Maybe you've put yourself right in the middle of it. Do you happen to remember your dreams?" asked Chase.

Silly had been picking up a pillow from the couch to hold in her lap, but when Chase asked about her dreams, she froze. He did know. How could anyone know? She hadn't even told her mother what she'd been dreaming about. And neither she and Rachel nor Julia had said anything to anyone about the necklace. Did he know about that as well? What was going on here? Silly took a deep breath and tried to organize her thoughts and remain calm as she spoke.

"Y-yes, Chase, I do remember my dreams. Lately, anyway. They've been particularly vivid. But I don't understand. How can you know anything about them? What's the real reason you're here in my living room right now?" Silly asked. She hoped her desperate desire to find some kind of answer didn't show in her voice.

Chase sat back down on the couch and looked Silly in the eyes.

"I'm not who you think I am. I'm not just some high school kid who moved here because my parents got a decent job offer. I can see things, and they can see me. Does that scare you?" Chase asked.

"It would have, a few weeks ago, but now, I don't know if anything you say could scare me more than I already am. Do you know what I've been dreaming about? Did you see that? What kinds of things do you see?" Silly's interest was growing, and a small hope that Chase could actually turn out to be the answer to her prayers bloomed into life in her heart.

"Silly, it's a long story, and I know I've interrupted your dinnertime with your family. Can I just tell you that there are other worlds, other dimensions, and sometimes things can leak through from there into our world? Would you believe something like that?" It didn't really seem to be a question, Silly realized. Chase already knew that she would believe it. Somehow, Silly knew that Chase was being completely honest with her.

"I think you know that I would believe that. I think you have some knowledge about what's been going on that no one else does, and I would really, really like it if you could share that with me. I would really, really like it if you could tell me that I'm not crazy, that this is really real," confessed Silly. It was hard for her to swallow past the lump in her throat. Suddenly, Silly laughed out loud.

"I'm sorry, I'm so sorry. I know laughing like that must make you think I'm absolutely crazy, but it's just that this feels like a dream. Not one of those horrible dreams, it's just I never thought that anyone in real life would ever have a conversation like this. It's so, I don't know, crazy." Silly laughed again, but not so heartily. This time was more in embarrassment. Chase was quick to reassure her.

"It's okay to laugh, Silly. There are a lot of bad things going on, but the only way we can beat them and take everything back to the way it was is to, first of all, be ourselves. Nobody can take everything seriously all the time; it's important to remember that. It's even more important to have faith that we can fix it, that everything can be okay. Can you do that?" Chase asked in the most serious tone of voice Silly had heard him use yet.

"That's the only thing that's kept me going so far. I think that if I ever stopped believing that there was the tiniest chance that everything would be okay eventually, I wouldn't be able to even get out of bed anymore," Silly honestly answered.

"Do you want to talk now? I can always make myself a sandwich later or something. I can go let my mom know, and she and my brother can finish eating without me. Would you like something to drink, or anything else?" Silly offered.

"If you're sure you're ready to talk now, that's fine with me. And I wouldn't turn down a nice cold glass of water," Chase smiled reassuringly at Silly.

Silly was amazed at how much better she felt about everything already. Chase's smile was like a healing balm. She smiled back at him, then stood up and returned to the dining room to talk to her mom and Justin.

"Mom, is it okay if I eat later? I really need to talk to Chase. He can help."

Rachel raised an eyebrow, and then understood what Silly meant. Justin was unaware of the situation at Julia's, and of Silly's worsening sleep problems. The same tiny spark of hope blossomed to life in Rachel's heart, and she eagerly nodded at Silly.

"Of course, Silly. Or would he like to join us? There's more than enough," Rachel suggested.

"Good idea, Mom. I'll ask," Silly brightened up even more at that idea.

She ran back out into the living room, where Chase was sitting patiently.

"What, you're out of water?" Chase joked.

"Oh! No, actually, my mom suggested that you might want to join us for dinner and we could maybe talk after? There's plenty to go around. And I think my mom would like to be part of this conversation that we're going to have, if that's okay with you. Is it?" Silly paused, unsure about whether or not it would be okay with her, let alone with Chase.

"I would love to," Chase replied. "And if you are comfortable with your mother being part of this conversation, that would be fine with me. Although, I would like to get to know the two of you a bit first, so that makes the dinner idea even better."

Chase got up, and Silly led him into the dining room, where she pointed him to the chair with no place setting. Silly went into the kitchen to get a plate and silverware, along with a glass of ice water for Chase. Arms full, she brought it all into the dining room and first set the glass in front of him so he could have a drink.

"I hope you like spaghetti, Chase. Would you like to start with some salad?" asked Rachel.

"Thank you, Mrs. Sharp. I'd love some salad. I really appreciate your inviting me to join you. That's very thoughtful of you."

"Please, Chase, call me Rachel. It seems like we're going to get to know each other well, so let's just start off pretending we're old friends," suggested Rachel.

Justin stared at his mother. He'd never known her to volunteer that one of her children's' friends call her by her first name, even Julia, who she'd known practically forever. There was definitely something fishy going on here, and Justin was not going to let another thing slide by without knowing the whole story.

Silly was also temporarily taken aback, but then she realized that her mother was only trying to put everyone at ease. Still, what would Justin think? As Silly was about to open her mouth, Rachel spoke again.

"And I think it's time the whole family had some idea of what's going on. Justin, I know how smart you are. I also know how curious you are, and when you're suspicious that someone's hiding something from you, you won't stop until you figure it out," Rachel paused to take a deep breath. "The truth is, something strange is going on with Silly, and Chase is going to help us figure it out."

Everyone at the table turned their heads to look at Justin.

"What does this have to do with the woods?" asked Justin.

Chase laughed. "He is the smart one, isn't he? I'll bet you two ladies hadn't even realized yet that the woods have anything to do with your situation, have you?"

Rachel and Silly looked at each other, bewildered. Chase knew he was right, so he continued.

"I thought this was just going to be a nice peaceful meal, but I see now that I've underestimated the three of you. I'll start at the beginning, and you can ask questions as I talk, and I'll try to answer them, so that you won't forget anything by waiting until I'm finished. Does that sound like a plan to everyone?"

The family all nodded their agreement, and waited for Chase to take a bite before he began.

"This is wonderful, Rachel!" he cried, "but it's time to get down to business, isn't it? Once upon a time, in the far away land of New York

City, a boy was born with a special talent." Chase looked at the faces around the table, checking to see how his fairy tale approach would go over.

Rachel laughed. "Silly's been telling fairy stories that begin with 'once upon a time' her entire life, Chase, so I think you've won us over already."

Silly grinned, and then looked at her plate, slightly embarrassed. A boy is a boy, after all.

Chase was glad that he'd chosen the correct tactic on his first try.

"All right, then, all joking aside, as this is serious business, I'll go on with the story.

"Once upon a time, blah blah, I was born. As I grew up, bit by bit, my parents began to understand that there was something different about me. I was happy playing by myself most of the time, and I seemed to have quite a lot of imaginary friends. As they listened in on my play, they noticed different sets of friends. I had different sets depending on where we were, and none would really follow me on vacations or even day trips. I would gather a whole new set of friends everywhere I went. They weren't sure how to deal with that, weren't sure how normal I was. I'm sure you know, Rachel, parents worry incessantly about whether or not their children are going to be okay."

Rachel nodded knowingly.

"One of my father's colleagues at the university was a noted child psychologist, had written dozens of papers, and was very well-respected in his field. My father brought this up with him, and he said that while it's relatively uncommon, almost all children are aware of the differences in their surroundings, especially when they traveled as much as my family and I did. He didn't see a problem with it, since I was well ahead of the curve on many other levels of development.

"My parents tried to be relieved, but I could tell that they weren't. I tried to pretend that some of my friends were always with me, no matter where we went. Unfortunately, I tried too hard, and this sudden change, right on the heels of their discussion of my father's findings, added up to them as a conspiracy. Yes, I was conspiring at a young age to hide what I could do, as soon as I found out that not everyone could do it."

"But what exactly is it that you can do?" asked Justin, curiosity getting the better of his patience.

"You're right, Justin; I don't need to paint the whole picture of my childhood for you. What I can do is not like a new sense; I think it's something everyone could do if they focused on their own senses. I am aware of the people, places and things that surround all of us, every single day, but no one else pays attention to. It's like seeing ghosts, but they're not ghosts.

"Do any of you know anything about alternate universes or quantum physics? That's a lot more complicated than what I do, but it would make explain much simpler. No? That's okay.

"Take this dinner for an example. Rachel, you chose to make spaghetti for dinner tonight, right?"

Rachel nodded her head, believing she understood what Chase was about to explain, but dubious that it could possibly be true.

"That one choice, spaghetti, could have gone so many other ways, right? Even after the choice of spaghetti is made, there are dozens or hundreds of other miniscule choices that could have led to an entirely different outcome than what we're feasting on right now. The pot to boil the noodles. The level of water, salt or oil in the water, the amount of noodles, whether to fill the pot with hot or cold water, which burner to use, all these choices that no one pays any attention to in every day life because they just don't seem to be truly important. Are you with me so far?"

Everyone nodded in agreement. This was easy enough to understand. Actually, the three of them had contemplated the effect of various choices on their everyday life at some point, so they were already a step ahead of the explanation.

"Every time a choice is made, a new universe spins off from this one. And then each time a choice is made in each of those new universes, more and more spin off. Do you know what fractals are? When you take a square, for example, and replace each line of the square with a square, and each line of the new shape with a square, and so on, and so on, until you have such a complex shape that somehow still bears a resemblance to the original simple square? That's what happens every second of every day.

"And I am aware of them all," Chase paused to let his announcement sink in a bit. He made a small smile at the three looks of skepticism, and continued.

"Okay, that's not exactly true. There's no way I could possibly be aware of them all, at all times. There's no way I could know how many I'm really aware of. Sometimes there are little things I notice, like a person at a restaurant picking up their fork. At the same time I see them picking up a different fork, with the same arm. It's fainter, but quite real to me. Most of the time I can tune that kind of thing out, like how your brain edits out your nose. You see your nose all the time, but you don't notice it's there when you're looking at the world around you. You only notice when something calls your attention to your nose, like a bit of glitter or an eyelash.

"That's what it's like for me. I've learned to edit out the small differences and only notice the big ones. That's what we're dealing with here. It's a big one, and it's not a happy one."

Silly stirred the food around on her plate, not taking a bite. This is what she had been afraid of, that there was something horribly wrong, and she was at ground zero.

Rachel noticed the look on Silly's face, and reached to take her hand.

"We'll make it all better, Silly, I promise we will," she told her daughter.

Justin agreed wholeheartedly. But there was still the problem of what exactly it was that they planned to make all better. He decided to get that laid out on the table as well.

"It's great that you can help, but I still don't know what it is you're supposed to be helping with. What's this big problem that has Silly all wrapped up in itself? What's going on?" he asked.

Rachel and Chase turned their heads from Justin to look at Silly.

"You're right. This is my story to tell. And I think it's time to tell all the other parts that I've kept to myself so as not to worry you, Mom. I'm sorry, but I couldn't tell you everything, not until now," Silly was too ashamed to look her mother in the eyes.

"It's okay, Silly. I do understand about not wanting to worry other people, you know," Rachel responded.

Silly took a deep breath, and began to fill Justin in on what Rachel knew so far.

"When I went to Julia's apartment for her birthday, she found a necklace in the couch. She didn't recognize it, and I didn't either, at first. But when I took it from her to look at, it did look familiar, and then it hypnotized me, or something. I can only remember this feeling like being pulled toward something dark. Julia said that I was talking about how beautiful it was and that I looked right through her, like she wasn't even there. When I dropped it, I snapped out of it, and she stopped me from picking the necklace back up. That was when Mom called because she woke up with the feeling that something was wrong. When Mom came over and we told her what happened, none of us could find the necklace again, but the spot on the floor where Julia threw it was burned. Mom said it was the shape of me, and Julia saw a monster from when she was a kid. They wouldn't let me look at it. Then we came home."

Silly stopped, and looked back and forth between Chase and Justin. Justin looked really interested, but Chase was starting to look more and more afraid.

"Chase? What is it?" Silly asked, anxiously.

"I didn't see a necklace at all. I had no idea that it was back. I don't know that my plan is the right one, anymore," Chase stopped, and looked thoughtful.

"What do you mean, 'back?' Do you know what necklace I'm talking about? It had a red stone, and a spiral," Silly trailed off at the look of horror on Chase's face.

"Oh, no. Not the red stone. That's the worst of all. That means the beast is loose again, and—"Chase quickly stopped himself, but one glance around the table told him that he'd already said far too much.

"The beast?" asked Rachel and Silly, in unison.

Justin simply stared at Chase, waiting for him to go on. He had to go on.

"You're right. I have to go on. I can't believe I let that slip, but I never thought that—I never imagined—I can't believe this is happening. This is going to take a lot longer than I thought to explain.

"The necklace with the red stone is the key to the Labyrinth. No, I need to start farther back.

"Almost all of the fairy tales and mythology and folklore you have ever heard or read is true, somewhere, somewhen. Remember what I said about choices? There have been choices made for millions of years. There are many times many different universes, and anything you can imagine can happen in at least one of them. Vampires and werewolves, witches and warlocks, zombies and man-eating dinosaurs, all are real somewhere. It's when the universes connect again, through people like me, that these stories are created. Sometimes we're the defense, sometimes the offense.

"Just know that all of your dreams are true. Not just your happy daydreams, all of your dreams and worst nightmares. Including the Minotaur."

Chase paused to let that sink in for a moment. Rachel and Justin looked scared but still interested, but Silly seemed to be paralyzed with fear.

After a long moment, Silly spoke.

"Is that what's chasing me? In my dreams?" she asked.

"Yes,' replied Chase.

They sat in silence for a moment, letting that thought sink in. Then Chase continued.

"I know how horrible this must sound to you, but I have to explain that the monster isn't here yet. It's trying, as hard as it can, to get into this world, but all it's been able to do so far has been, well, the easiest way to explain it is to call it haunting. It's haunting those woods, and it's haunting you, Silly." Chase explained.

"What it needs is for Silly to have the necklace in her possession, for her to be kept under its spell long enough to open a doorway between our world and that one. Until that happens, it won't have a truly real presence here. As long as we can keep that from happening, this is as bad as things will get. I know it feels like they can't get any worse right now, but believe me, they can. They can get a lot worse."

"What do you mean? What can happen?" asked Silly.

"Well, right now, you feel like you're losing a lot of yourself because you can't get any restful sleep, am I right?" asked Chase.

Silly sighed. "You're exactly right. It's like the rest of the world is fuzzy, like my brain is always in a fog. I only really feel like myself when I'm having those dreams, but I can't continue to do this forever, Chase. I don't know how I can live like this much longer."

"That's what I'm here to help you with, Silly. I'm going to take you by the hand and walk you through each and every step you need to take to banish the Minotaur back to where it came from, banish it completely and forever, so that it can never, ever do this to you or to anyone else. We have to work together, but I can only teach you what you need to do. You're the one who's been chosen, and you're the one who will have to take the most risk. We will all be behind you, but when it comes down to it, you'll have to face the monster alone. I wish there was another way to do this, but if there is, I don't know what it is. I'm sorry, Silly. I'm so sorry," finished Chase.

Rachel's face had paled, and when she heard Chase apologize, that was the straw that broke the camel's back. She meant to use a more forceful tone, but when her words came out, they were only whispers.

"What do you mean, the most risk? What's going to happen to my daughter? Why can't anyone else help her with this?" Rachel asked.

"Well," began Chase, "she's the person who was chosen. I can't tell you why yet, but there's something Silly knows or feels that made her the most accessible target for the Minotaur. From what I've learned from trying to study everything I can about this, over my lifetime, it has a lot to do with imagination and creativity. Artists tend to see the world in ways that the average person doesn't, and that seems to have something to do with a latent ability to transcend this universe for others. Basically, Silly is a conduit for magic."

Chase chuckled to himself. It was always a new adventure explaining the life he led to others. At some point in the conversation, he always fell back on the same kind of story, the kind of story that mankind had shared for thousands of years. When something was just inexplicable, it became magic.

Silly nodded at Chase's explanation, and turned to her mother to comfort her.

"Mom, you know I've been telling fairy tales my entire life. I never thought to talk to you or anyone else about it. Sometimes it's like I'm being told these stories by someone else, like they're using my voice to talk or my hand to write. I feel like the stories are already there, waiting for me to come along and share them with the rest of the world. I don't even have to think about them, or about what's going to happen in them. They're already complete by the time I begin the telling. I think that's what Chase means about me being a conduit. The stories come through me, and I am an artist. My art is the fairy tale," Silly finished.

"But Silly, you were telling stories as soon as you could talk. I think you were telling them before then, even. I know you told me stories with your eyes and your baby smile. You were such a charming baby, and you still are. You're enchanting," Rachel trailed off, not knowing what point she was trying to make with her speech.

"I don't think I'm enchanting, Mom. I think I'm enchanted. That's what we're trying to tell you. All this, everything that I've been going through, is because of my fairy tales. It's because of magic. I know that has to be hard for you to swallow, but that's the way it is. That's the way I am," Silly said.

Silly got out of her chair and walked around the table to give her mother a hug.

"I know you're really worried about me, and I was really worried too, until Chase came over and started to explain everything. But I understand a lot more than what he's told us. I understand a lot more than you give me credit for. I know it must be hard to see your babies grow up and not need you anymore, but I do need you. I'll always need you. But this is something I have to fix by myself. You can't see the things I see. I don't want you to see them. They're horrible things, Mom. You've suffered enough. It's time to let go. It's time to let me grow up," finished Silly.

Chase nodded his approval. Choosing Silly had been the Minotaur's last mistake. She was exactly the kind of person who could end his depredations once and for all. She was smart, strong, and above all, she believed in herself. He knew that they still had a long, hard road ahead of them, but he could not be happier with the companion he had been given.

"I think I need to talk to Chase alone now. Mom, Justin? Do you mind if we sit in here alone and finish talking?" asked Silly.

"Sure thing, Silly. Just don't keep secrets from me anymore, okay?" grinned Justin.

Rachel wasn't so sure.

"Silly, I don't know about this. I just—I just don't know," she trailed off into silence, looking at her daughter's face for what she feared would be one of the last times.

"Mom, things are going to be okay. Things are going to be better than okay. I promise. Everything will be okay. I love you, Mom," Silly smiled.

"I love you too, Silly," responded Rachel. She slowly stood up and made her way into her bedroom. Justin followed her down the hall and went into his own room.

When the sounds of footsteps and doors opening and closing had faded, Silly returned to her chair, sat down, and looked Chase straight in the eyes.

"Tell me what I need to do," she simply said, and waited for his answer.

"It's not as easy as that, Silly. I wish it was, but it's not. We have a lot of background to go over before we can even start thinking about what we need to do. But I'm willing to work hard, and I know now that you are too. So let's get started.

"I don't know how familiar you are with the Greek Minotaur, but I'll summarize what's pertinent to our story today. The Minotaur was a monster with the body of a man and the head of a bull. He was born from his mother, who had been forced to fall in love with a bull. Because of this, he needs to feast on human flesh to sustain his life. He was imprisoned in a labyrinth, which he roamed for many, many years. In some worlds, he was finally killed by a hero without ever escaping, but in the world this Minotaur comes from, he killed and ate every hero who ever attempted to slay him, and eventually grew large and strong enough to break free of his stone prison.

"After he escaped, he was still trapped on the island of Crete, but he managed to subdue his natural killing instinct for long enough to make his way onto a ship bound for the mainland. When land was in sight, he massacred the ship's entire crew and swam the rest of the way to shore. He roamed the countryside for dozens of years, killing when he was hungry, and sleeping wherever he grew tired.

"Finally, an evil sorceress found a way to keep him from murdering, at least, in that world. She created a talisman from a tiny piece of a magical red stone. She put spells upon spells on the stone, and bound them all together with gold and silver wire, wrapping around and around the stone in a spiral that connected to itself, making it never-ending. She attached a chain to it and set out to find the monster's lair. As I said, the Minotaur travelled far and wide, and didn't have a permanent home. The sorceress tracked him for many years before coming close enough to put her plan into action.

"She watched as he destroyed entire villages, leaving no living person behind. She watched and waited. Finally, he began to grow tired, and lay down to sleep in a field far from any source of food. The sorceress crept up on him as he slept, and chanting her final incantations, threw the chain over his head with the last of her strength.

"The sudden movement woke him, but before he could murder the sorceress for what she had done, he began to fade out of that world. He faded until he was merely a shadow, unable to do physical harm to any living thing. The Minotaur realized what she had done, and he tore at his chest, trying to remove her talisman. The witch had foreseen this, and made sure to add enough spells to prevent him from being able to remove it on his own.

"The only way the necklace could be removed from the neck of the Minotaur was by a mortal human's hand. For many more years he tried to escape from between all worlds into one, any one, one where he could trick some poor hapless soul into taking his necklace from him. Finally, the Minotaur discovered the means to end his imprisonment.

"He'd spent such a long time between worlds that he had learned how to manipulate time and space in certain places, and the more he practiced, the better he became at it. He learned that he could force just enough of his spirit into a world to take the shape of the talisman, and tempted the first person to find it into picking it up and putting it on. As soon as that person put the necklace on, it became the talisman from the neck of the Minotaur, and he was released into that world to wreak havoc again.

"The sorceress had been unaware that she had left any loopholes for the monster to escape, and she was long dead by the time he discovered the secret, so she could not undo his damage a second time. However, she'd left a careful record of the spells she'd placed on the stone, and the process that she'd used to bind it into permanence with the gold and silver wire. The only problem was that her records were in one world, while the Minotaur was loose in another.

"The solution was people like me. We searched and searched until we found the Minotaur's origin, and studied her spells and compared them with the weakness that had been revealed. The world which the Minotaur was exploring was coming closer and closer to total destruction, and we didn't have much time left. We learned that if the Minotaur did not leave anyone to place the talisman back around his neck, he would be trapped on that world for the rest of his life.

"Still, that solution left too much to chance. There was no way to know who would find the necklace one day, and achieve the same thing the sorceress had, to come upon the monster while he slept and chain him again. We had to take matters into our own hands.

"A volunteer was chosen to do what the Minotaur had done, to extend a part of himself into another world, with a single purpose: to find and destroy the talisman.

"It took longer to find than we had expected. Many host bodies died before the volunteer finally found the talisman. He was armed with the words he needed to destroy its magic, and the special container that we had made which he would seal the red stone in to make sure it was never found again.

"We did not know that our volunteer had had a change of heart. As we all waited for him to say the words and seal the stone away for all eternity, he brought the rest of his essence into that other world, and escaped us. He hunted down the Minotaur and somehow reasoned with the beast, who allowed our man to put the necklace back around his hairy neck. The Minotaur faded again, but this time, he knew what he had to do to escape, this time, and every time, because he also knew that he had to find someone else to put the necklace back on him so he could travel again.

"But we had found our flaw. If the necklace was instead replaced by the same person who had removed it, the Minotaur would be destroyed forever. And, I'm sorry, Silly, but that's where you come in. You have to take the necklace again. You have to pick it up, and put it around your neck. And then you have to take it off and put it back on the monster. That is the only way to end this," Chase finished.

"Oh," said Silly, in the smallest voice she'd ever heard. "Oh."

"I know, from what I've told you, this must sound like certain death, but it's not. I promise you with everything I have that it's not. I'm here to help you, and you can do this. I promise," vowed Chase.

"But, wait. You keep saying 'we' as if you were around for all of that, as if you were in on it too. You weren't, were you? I mean, you said all that earlier about your parents, and, I mean, you're from New York. What's really going on here?" asked Silly, confused. It was easier for her to focus on the inconsistencies in Chase's story than the fantastic chore he had just assigned to her and her alone.

"Um, about that—I lied to you earlier. I can't tell all of this to everyone I come across. It's too much for most people to believe. Your mother isn't going to take the truth well, so I saved her from having to deal with it at all. I'm 1700 years old, Silly. My kind lives for thousands of years, just so that we can handle crises like this. We have to be able to find solutions and follow through on them, and that just can't be done within the meager span of a normal human lifetime. Sorry about that," Chase apologized.

Silly could only stare, with her mouth open. So many thoughts whirled through her mind at this moment; she couldn't choose the first one to speak aloud. But finally she did.

"But what about high school? Why would you be a kid? Why not a grown up? Wouldn't you be able to do so much more as an adult than as a kid? I mean, look at me, I can't do anything, because I'm a kid!" Silly's voice rose and rose, until Chase hushed her so as not to disturb Rachel.

"Because of you, Silly. Because of you. I had to get close to you. What would your mother have thought if a grown man came knocking on your door and asked to see you alone? Would she have let me in or would she have called the cops? It's not always best to be an adult. Sometimes you can get more done as a kid," Chase explained.

That did seem to make much more sense to Silly. She wished she'd have thought about that before she got so upset, and blurted everything out, louder and louder. She paused to consider what real questions she had for Chase, what questions she needed answered if she were to be able to do what she had to do. She took a deep breath to clear her mind of all distractions, and focus on her task.

"Okay, Chase, exactly how am I supposed to put this necklace on again? I haven't seen it since the one time at Julia's apartment. Is there some way of calling it to me?" she asked, all business again.

"That's what we have to work on right now. I need you to tell me what you've been dreaming about the necklace. Once I know that, it will be easier to figure out what we need to do to make it come back to you again," said Chase.

"Okay, but the only thing I ever dream about is what happened that night I touched it. We're sitting on the couch, and then Julia handed me the necklace, and it was like I went away down a deep, dark hole and I waited at the bottom until it fell out of my hand," Silly told Chase.

He seemed surprised. "That's all? You don't dream about it calling to you or finding it anywhere else? That seems strange," he finished in an aside to himself. Chase tapped his finger against his chin as he thought.

"Well, while I'm in the darkness, it's like the darkness is all around me, but it can't touch me yet. And I hear these strange noises, the sounds around me in the dark. Like shuffling sounds. They're really scary. Oh! And I hear you calling me," said Silly.

"You—you hear me? You hear my voice? Are you sure it's me?" Chase asked, very curious.

"Yes, I didn't know it was you until you came to the door tonight, but it's definitely you. I wasn't even aware that anyone was calling me for weeks, but lately, I've been trying to concentrate in my dreams, if that makes any sense. And I finally heard you. Well, I heard a voice, and it turned out to be you. Just calling my name."

Chase and Silly looked at each other across the table for a long minute. Finally, Chase cleared his throat and spoke again.

"Silly, this is not at all what anyone expected. You're—well, you're the person we've been looking for. You really are the one who can defeat the Minotaur, and you probably didn't even need our help in the first place," Chase stopped at the look on Silly's face.

"I don't understand, Chase. I didn't even start having these dreams until after I picked up the necklace. I wasn't having any of the chasing dreams until after you were already here. Why would you come if—" Silly broke off. There had been something, before Chase came. There had been a dream. She tried and tried to remember.

"Oh! I know you. I do know you. I dreamed you, before you came. You were a knight riding a white horse, and you came to save me from a monster. I remember. It was you," she said.

Chase was stunned. He didn't know what to make of the situation anymore. There was no way Silly could have dreamed of him, not before he'd shown up here. There was no way at all. Unless...

"Silly, you said that your stories are already told, didn't you? They come to you whole, and you just write them down or tell them, you don't have to think about it at all, is that right?" Chase asked.

"Of course. That's how it's always been for me. Why do you ask?" Silly was confused, now.

"Silly, you're one of us. You've been making contact with the other worlds all your life, and you've done it without any help from any of us. You're the only person who's ever been able to do that. I don't know how this is going to affect our battle with the Minotaur, but I'm going to find out. I think it can only mean good things for us. I think this will make it much, much easier to beat him," Chase said.

Silly was in awe of what Chase was telling her. She didn't know what to do or what to say. She was magic? Silly let out a nervous chuckle.

"So I'm going to live for thousands of years?" she asked, only half jokingly.

"I can't say for sure, but if you really are one of us, and it sure sounds like you are, then probably so," answered Chase.

Silly marveled for a moment at this change of fortune, and then turned her thoughts back to the present.

"Never mind, Chase, that's not what's important right now. What's important is stopping the monster before he can hurt anyone else, in this world or any other. We have to stop him forever. What do I need to do?" she asked.

"Thank you, Silly, for having your priorities straight while I'm sitting here baffled by what you just told me. Here's what you need to do tonight. When you have the dream about the necklace, try to hold on to it. Try to put it around your own neck—" Chase broke off as Silly interrupted him.

"But I'm never really holding it. When I go down the hole, I don't have it, and I can see myself still holding it at the other end of the tunnel, but I don't have it. The part of me that's thinking and real in the dream doesn't have the necklace at all. And what about my other dream? I know it's about the Minotaur, now. It's chasing me through the woods. I run and run through the whole dream, but it never catches me. Should I—stop?" asked Silly.

"Silly," began Chase, shaking his head, "sometimes I wonder if you're more trouble than you're worth."

Silly looked at him in shock.

"Okay, that's not what I really think. What I'm trying to say is that everything we've planned for has turned out to be wrong. I'm going to have to start all over in working this out so we can beat the monster once and for all. You don't hold the necklace in your dream, and he's actually chasing you in another?" Chase asked.

"Yes. Those are the bad ones. The necklace dreams don't bother me. I think if I only had those, I wouldn't be in the position that I'm in now. It's the chasing dreams that have hurt me so badly. Those are the dreams that I need to stop if I'm going to have any kind of life left. Please, Chase, should I stop and let him catch me? What would happen then?" Silly was very insistent.

"Silly, I just don't know. I can't tell you to do that. I can't even suggest it as a good idea. There's a chance that if he catches you in a dream, since you can travel somehow between the worlds, that act could free him into this world. And I don't want you to get hurt. I don't want to lose you," Chase was growing more and more upset at just the thought of Silly being harmed by the beast.

"Okay, Chase. I won't do that. I promise," Silly said aloud as she thought to herself, I don't always keep my promises.

Chase heaved a sigh of relief. He put his hands to the table and pushed himself back in his chair.

"Silly, I need to go home. I've got a lot of thinking to do, and I think you do, too. I have to come up with some way for us to fight the

Minotaur, now that I know our previous plan is not going to work. Can I come back in the morning to talk to you some more?" Chase asked.

"Sure," Silly shrugged. "I don't have anything going on, besides my newfound mission to save the world."

They laughed together, and Silly walked Chase to the front door and let him out.

"I'll see you tomorrow, Silly," said Chase.

Silly smiled at him, and nodded.

Twenty-Four

"Some promises are made to be broken," Silly whispered to herself as she walked down the hall to her bedroom. She could hear the sound of her mother lightly snoring in her own bedroom, and all was quiet behind Justin's door. That was just as well; Silly didn't want anyone to tell her not to do what she was about to be doing.

Once she was in her room, Silly sat on her bed and asked herself if she really wanted to do this. She thought for a few minutes, and then nodded to herself. Yes. She was going to do this, and no one was going to stop her. She stood up with new determination, and picked out her most comfortable pajamas. She pulled back her covers and started to get into bed, then stopped herself. One more thing.

Silly put on a pair of socks, and tied her running shoes tightly to her feet. Then she slid under the covers and pulled them up to her neck. She nestled her head comfortably into her pillow, and closed her eyes.

Silly slipped into slumber as if it were an old friend, not the enemy that it had become over the past few weeks. She welcomed sleep this night. She embraced it. And so began her dreams.

Again she was sitting on Julia's couch; again Julia found the necklace and handed it to Silly. But this time, instead of slipping away into that dark hole as she had every other time, Silly squeezed her eyes tightly shut, clamped her fist closed around the necklace, and concentrated with everything she had on staying here, on remaining in Julia's living room.

Slowly, she opened her eyes to take a peek.

Julia was no longer sitting next to her. In her place was a strange, small woman, who looked to be just entering middle age. While no longer exactly young, the woman was stunningly beautiful, and Silly's heart ached to look like that, for just one day. The woman turned her head in Silly's direction and smiled with half of her mouth before speaking.

"I believe you have something there that belongs to me," she said.

Silly was afraid to open her mouth. This was the sorceress Chase had told her about. This was the woman who had caused every problem that Silly had had this summer. This woman was the cause of death of millions upon millions of people. This woman was pure evil.

"I see you already know who I am; at least, you think you do. Let me introduce myself. My name is Unduire. I have certain abilities. I used nearly all of them in the creation of that which you hold in your hand at this very moment. Perhaps you would like to hear a bit more about my achievements."

"I—I do know who you are. You made this talisman to capture the Minotaur, to stop him from killing everyone in your world. Why are you here now? What are you planning to do?" boldly asked Silly.

Unduire laughed loudly, throwing her head back to expose her snow white neck. She tossed her copper hair behind her shoulders and smiled fully at Silly this time.

"Is that what he told you? Is that what you think? No. I did indeed make my talisman to capture the Minotaur, but not from some silly sense of righteousness. No, I meant to capture him and use him for my own plans. He was to be my pet, you see. My pet and my weapon against all who stood in my way. He did well for a very long time, until those whimpering fools meddled in my plans. He never escaped, as they may have told you. I see that they did. He never escaped. This has been my plan all along. To let them believe that I was doing my world a service. To let them believe that there was some small bit of good in my heart.

"They were wrong. There is not now, nor has there ever been, the slightest bit of kindness or weakness inside me. I sent the Minotaur between the worlds. I set him free again. I let them execute their plans to thwart him. I had to wait, you see, until you came along, my darling."

Silly began to shiver, although it hadn't been cold that night, on Julia's birthday. It didn't feel cold now, but her teeth began to chatter.

Unduire continued to smile at Silly's discomfort. It seemed that the more uncomfortable Silly became, the more comfortable Unduire became. Her smile broadened.

"Do you dream about my pet, my dear? I think that you do. I think you have been dreaming about him for quite some time now. Have you let him catch you yet? No, of course not. You're a good girl, aren't you? You'd never let some mean old beastie catch you." Unduire laughed again.

"What a lovely surprise you're in for, darling."

Silly woke and sat bolt upright in her bed. She had sweated through her pajamas, and a scream was trapped in her throat. She had to talk to Chase, and now. This couldn't wait for tomorrow. The evil sorceress hadn't died. She was still alive, and they were playing right into her hands! But—were they? Silly couldn't imagine someone as carefully crafty as Unduire letting on that Silly and Chase were making such a big mistake. She wouldn't take a chance of anything messing up her grand plans for the Minotaur, would she? It had to be another trick.

Silly let her arms collapse beneath her, and fell back onto her pillow. What should she do? She couldn't decide whether or not Unduire had told her what she did so that Silly would tell Chase or keep it to herself. She turned her head to look at the clock on her bedside table. It wasn't even midnight yet.

Silly told herself no very firmly. No, she didn't need to breathe a word of this to Chase. Besides, it wasn't even midnight yet. She'd go back to sleep and see what happened. She'd see which dream she would have, and maybe just stick with her original plan of letting the Minotaur catch her. That way, it would be like she'd never even woken up.

It took a long time before her heart slowed down to a more normal pace instead of feeling like it was about to beat out of her chest, but finally, Silly was calm and relaxed again. She closed her eyes and lay in bed, waiting for sleep to come. Unfortunately, her mind refused to slow down and let her body sleep. She kept wondering if what she was doing was the right thing or not. She kept wondering if she would be able to sleep at all. It had been so long since Silly had not fallen asleep as soon as her head hit the pillow, she couldn't remember what steps she used to take to go to sleep. As she debated on the benefits of counting sheep, she actually fell asleep.

Silly opened her eyes in a new dream. She had expected to either return to Julia's living room or be running through the woods, but this was a new, strange place. She stood on a rocky plateau, not far from a steep drop-off. As she looked down at herself, she marveled at the strange clothes she was wearing. They reminded her of a Renaissance fair she'd once been to on a school field trip. It was a long, dark green dress, with long sleeves that puffed at the shoulders. There were many long hours' worth of embroidery on the bodice, in beautiful colors and dazzling designs. Sill was so distracted by the dress that she didn't hear the first step from behind her, but the second caught her attention, and she whirled around.

"Welcome to my home," said Unduire.

Silly stared at the sorceress. Even though Unduire was such a terrible person, Silly couldn't help but admire her physical beauty, and the confident way in which she approached Silly.

"I knew you wouldn't tell that other little fool that you'd talked to me. I knew you couldn't resist trying to take care of things all by your little lonesome. I'm ever so glad of that. You haven't failed me yet, my darling, and I don't believe that you ever will," Unduire smiled at Silly.

"Why am I here?" asked Silly, trying to beat the witch at her game.

"You're here because I wish you to be, of course. We need to talk a little more, and I'm much more comfortable in my home than yours. I also took the liberty of dressing you, as your other clothing was, hm, shall I say, inappropriate."

Unduire made a sweeping gesture with her arm, waving at the desolate land surrounding the two of them.

"Take a look around, my dear. This is what my pet will leave of your world when you fail to stop him as you plan. Isn't it beautiful? Listen to the silence. Breathe the still air. Bask in the solitude. This is what all worlds are meant to be, blank slates for me, and a few others like me, to design on them what we wish," said Unduire.

Silly turned a bit to her left, because she did want to look around, not because Unduire had told her to do so. As far as her eyes could see, there were no birds in the air, no animals on the ground, and no signs of human habitation.

"Is it like this—everywhere?" Silly asked.

"Of course. In order to make my own version of paradise, I had to first remove every trace of what anyone else had ever done. I had to remove every living thing and every sign that they had ever existed. Quite an accomplishment, if I do say so myself. It took many years of learning and incantations, many searches for special items that would help me. But now, I am finished. With this world, at least," Unduire smiled at Silly.

"But I don't understand," said Silly, confused. "I thought people like you needed others to control. Why would you wipe out everyone and everything?"

"You don't understand because you're only a mere mortal, my darling. I don't need anything. I only want, and I only take what I want. What I want is to be alone. When I have conquered the worlds that I want, ii will no longer even need my pet. He has served me well, and I do know how to be merciful, although I do not make it a habit to practice mercy of any kind. He will be rewarded as only I can reward him," explained Unduire.

Silly thought she was beginning to understand.

"You really don't want control over anyone. You just want to be the only person left. That's the ultimate control, isn't it? Deciding that everyone else's life is going to end, and being the one to end them. This is wrong, this is evil. You're not going to do this. I'm not going to let you. I'm going to stop you, but first I'm going to stop your monster. You're not going to win this time!" screamed Silly, completely unafraid in her defiance. She could feel the blood rushing to her face as she screamed louder and louder, her hands clenched into fists at her sides.

Silly took one step toward Unduire, then another, and then stopped. Unduire laughed at this little girl who thought she could do anything.

"You're nobody. You're a toy. You'll never do anything to me," said Unduire.

Silly opened her mouth to deny everything that Unduire said, but felt herself fading away. She lifted a hand to her face, and was amazed to discover that she could see right through herself. The world around her was growing dark, and the last sound she heard was Unduire's hearty laugh. Everything faded into complete blackness, surrounding her on all sides.

Silly wondered if she was in the tunnel she went to in her dream while she held the necklace, but this felt different. She put a hand up and felt a wall to her right. When she raised her other hand, there was a wall on that side as well. Silly stood up, panic rising in her throat. She spun around, feeling the same rough stone walls on all sides of her, and above her, higher than she could reach. She was trapped.

Even though she was seriously concerned about the situation she'd gotten herself into, Silly kept her cool and reminded herself that this was still a dream, no matter how real it seemed. It wasn't reality yet.

She was trapped at the bottom of a well, or maybe an oubliette. She knew the stone walls went all the way around her without a break other than the cracks between the stones, but what about the floor? She knelt and felt around the entire floor, which was smooth and cold underneath a thin layer of dead leaves. Dead leaves? That was the key. There must be an opening above her to the outside, or else the leaves wouldn't have been able to fall in, right?

Silly stood back up and craned her neck to see if she could see any small speck of light above her, a single star, even. As she maintained that position, her eyes became adjusted to the darkness, and there seemed to be a lighter area high above her. The longer she stared, the more distinct it became. Yes! That just had to be the sky. Silly hoped she was right in thinking that if there was a way in, there had to be a way out.

She felt around the walls again, making sure she couldn't feel the shape of a doorway. Just as she checked the sky again, she saw a dark spot creep into the lighter area, right at the edge.

"Silly, you just won't listen, will you?" Chase called down to her.

"Chase! How did you find me? Are you in my dream or are you real?" Silly asked.

"I'm real, all right. I couldn't trust your promise to leave well enough alone, so I knew I'd better check in on you. I'll throw down this rope and help you climb out," said Chase.

Silly could barely make out what was going on high above her head, but she waited patiently until the end of the rope slapped against one of her outstretched arms. She pulled enough down to wrap around her body and tie securely in a knot, and then called up to Chase that she was ready.

"Okay, Silly, I'm going to pull, but it'll go much faster if you walk yourself up the sides. I'll keep tension in the rope so you won't fall if you slip, but give me a warning if you feel yourself slide so I can brace myself," Chase instructed.

Silly nodded, and then realized that chase couldn't see her down at the bottom, so she shouted up to him an affirmative. She grabbed the rope with both hands and leaned her back against one wall while she braced her feet on the other side. Step by step, she inched her way up the walls, keeping a steady pace.

It seemed like forever, but in just a few minutes, Chase was helping Silly out of the top of the well. They collapsed to the ground side by side, and looked at each other.

"Thank you for coming for me, Chase," said Silly. "I don't know how I would have gotten myself out of this without your help. How did you find me?"

"Ever since the first time I saw you, Silly, I've felt this connection to you. I'm drawn to you like a magnet. I'm always, always aware of you when I'm close enough. When you made that promise tonight, before I left, that you'd leave well enough alone, I knew you were lying. I went home knowing that you'd end up in big trouble without me, so when I went to sleep, I came looking for you in your dreams," said Chase.

Silly was glad of the darkness, because she was blushing.

"Chase, I've felt it too. That first day, even though you didn't really talk to me, I knew there was something there. I've tried to deny it ever since, but I can't do it anymore. I know we're meant to be together. Is that crazy?" Silly asked.

"It's not crazy at all. I'm glad, because without that, you could have been lost forever."

"Forever? What about when I wake up in the morning?" Silly asked.

"Silly, this is it. This is the battle. If we don't beat the Minotaur, nobody's going to wake up, ever again," said Chase.

"But what about Unduire?" asked Silly, giving voice to her fears. "There's so much more going on than just the Minotaur now. She's back, and she's been controlling him all along. And controlling you and your friends. What are we going to do about her?"

Chase gasped. "How do you know that name? I made sure to never tell you that name."

"She's here, Chase, I'm trying to tell you that. She was in my first dream when I went to sleep, my necklace dream. And I woke up and went back to sleep, and I was in a new dream, in her world. You have to believe me, Chase, because I believe her. She's here," Silly finished, wondering how she was going to convince Chase of this very real danger that they were both now in.

"She was in your dream? Did she talk to you? Did you talk to her? Oh, Silly, this keeps getting worse and worse. You can't listen to a word she says. She always tells the truth, but she always twists it so what you think she's saying isn't what she's really telling you. You have to tell me what she said," begged Chase.

"She told me I was playing into her hand, that we all were. Me, you, your friends, and everyone else. She wants to destroy everything, Chase. She wants to be alone," Silly explained.

"Silly, I—it doesn't matter what she said. I didn't even need to ask. Our priority right now is still the Minotaur. No matter what her real plans are, he's the first step. He's the key right now, and we have to stop him. We'll talk about her later. Right now, we have to focus on the beast," said Chase.

Silly stared in disbelief for a moment, but then quickly realized that Chase was absolutely right. The Minotaur was a direct threat to her world right now. He may be only a weapon, but he was a terrible one indeed.

"You're right, Chase," Silly agreed. "What do we have to do to beat this monster?"

"First we have to find him. Do you recognize this place at all from any of your dreams?" Chase asked.

Silly looked around. It was still very dark, but she thought the woods that they were in looked somewhat familiar. She stood up to get a better look, and gasped in surprise.

"These are the woods next door. I never knew there was an abandoned well here. Wait, is this really the woods, or are they different because I'm dreaming?" Silly looked to Chase for an answer.

"No, Silly, from now on, you can assume that everything you see is exactly how it is in real life. I told you, this is the battle. This is it," said Chase.

Silly nodded to Chase, and started walking in one direction, finding her way by choosing a tree and heading towards it, then choosing another, all in as straight a line as she could manage.

"Where's you get your forestry skills," asked Chase, impressed.

"My mom insisted we know how to get out of the woods since we had some right next door. This is for sure a small enough area that even from the center, it won't take long to make our way all the way out, and then I'll be able to tell you which side we're on, and we can begin the search wherever you think best," Silly explained.

Chase nodded, and then concentrated on just following Silly. He'd spent so many years in the city, he didn't know one tree from the next anymore, so he thought it best to keep his mouth shut and keep up.

It wasn't long at all before the two of them were walking through sparser, smaller trees, and then came out into a wide, cleared area.

"This is the back of the woods, if you're looking at them from the road," Silly declared. "Where are we going to start searching for the beast?"

"Let's walk around to the side that butts up against the apartment complex," decided Chase. "We can start from there. That's where I've always gone in to search for it, so I can direct you away from the areas I know he's never been."

"I thought you were prone to getting lost in the woods," said Silly. "How is it that you could search for the beast alone without any problems before?"

Chase shrugged, embarrassed. "Well, I guess I can admit this to you. I tied a piece of string to the first tree and unrolled it behind me as I explored. Hey, it worked in the labyrinth!"

Silly laughed.

"I'm glad you can still have a little bit of fun at my expense while our lives are at stake, and the lives of everyone we've ever met!" chided Chase.

They walked in companionable silence for almost the entire way around the woods, until they reached the parking lot. Chase turned to Silly, all seriousness.

"Silly, this is going to be very dangerous, and it may take a long, long time. Are you prepared for that?" he asked.

"I'm as ready as I'll ever be, Chase. Let's go," she replied.

Each held out a hand to the other, and they clasped them tightly together. As one, they reentered the woods, perhaps for the final time.

As Chase started to tell Silly which directions he'd explored, she stopped him from talking.

"I know which way to go. I know where he is. I can feel him," she explained.

Chase looked at her with worry in his eyes, but simply nodded and walked along with her in the direction that she pulled. As they walked, the lights from the parking lot faded until they were nearly in complete darkness again. This time, however, Silly's eyes had had a chance to adjust, and she could see perfectly well. They walked until they finally came to a small natural clearing that Silly knew to be near to the center of the woods.

Silly paused at the edge of the clearing, and Chase came up beside her to look. Both of them knew to stay quiet, even though there was nothing to be seen.

Yet.

And now we wait, they thought, simultaneously.

Chase wondered at the connection that Silly had to the beast. He'd never gotten to hear about her other dream, the one in which she was chased mercilessly through the forest. He would have known that dream was going to come true. He would never have let things get this far.

Silly knew what was coming next. She'd never dreamed this part, but it felt right. It felt like the part of the dream that she always came in after. This was the beginning, she knew. She knew she would shortly be running for her life, but she remained calm and unafraid.

Still they waited. Had it been minutes, or hours? Neither knew. Neither cared. They waited.

Suddenly, the clearing seemed to grow brighter. The two of them held their breath as the brightness grew in front of them. A shape began to form in the center of the clearing. At first it was just a darker mass in the center of the brightness, but then it began taking a more recognizable shape. It rose to stand on two legs like a man, but the head was horribly misshapen.

Chase and Silly both recognized the monster. The darkness of the shape changed to reveal its features, and Silly gasped to finally see the thing that had been haunting her for all this time. It looked up and turned its head to stare directly at her. Although it didn't have eyes yet, Silly felt its stare, deep in her bones. Chase turned to look at Silly for what he feared would be the last time. He squeezed her hand, and felt her let go. He waited to see what she was doing.

Silly took a step forward, into the clearing.

The Minotaur, now fully formed and completely in this world, turned his body to face her. His glowing red eyes locked with Silly's pale blue ones. In that moment, they knew what was going to happen. He threw his bull's head back and roared, shaking the leaves from the trees surrounding the clearing.

Silly turned to her left and took off running, as fast as she could. She didn't spare a second to look at Chase, to tell him goodbye. She put everything she had into her two feet, and ran as though her life depended on it.

The Minotaur didn't give Chase a glance; he took off after Silly almost at the same instant that she began her run. His feet pounded the ground, shaking it until Chase didn't know if he would be able to stay upright. Chase wondered at Silly's bravery, or was it only foolishness? He hoped desperately that he would find out which it was.

As the sound and shaking of the Minotaur's chase faded from Chase's hearing, he wondered what he should do, what Silly's plan was. He took a step into the clearing, hoping that it would help to clear his head as well.

He looked down at the ground in the place that the Minotaur had appeared, and there, right before him in the leaf litter, he saw a glint of gold winking at him in the moonlight. Chase knelt to investigate, and after sweeping the leaves to the side, he was shocked to discover the talisman that he had been warned about his entire life. He didn't dare to touch it to pick it up, but he could examine all he wanted without touching. The red stone was darkly mysterious, and seemed to call to him to touch it, to stroke it, to verify its reality. The gold and silver wire binding it into place spiraled infinitely, winding around and around.

Chase shook his head violently and fell backwards onto the ground. He's nearly picked the necklace up. It was so mesmerizing; he didn't know what he should do with it. If he put it on, the Minotaur would be called back to this spot, away from chasing Silly. But Chase wasn't the one that had to beat the monster; that was Silly's destiny. Chase had never wished so badly for his mentor since the man had changed sides in the last fight with the Minotaur. Even if he was on the side of evil and destruction, it would feel safer to ask someone who had such a massive wealth of knowledge on this subject.

Chase dared to take one more look at the talisman as it lay on the ground in front of him. That stone. It was so beautiful, and yet, somehow, familiar. Where had he seen something like that before?

Chase's memory flashed backward, through all the hundreds of years he'd lived. He remembered once, when he was really a child, there had been a woman leaning over him in his bed. She had a pendant swinging gently from a fine silver chain that hung around her neck, with a darkly gleaming red stone set in the center. It was the same stone, but the gold and silver wire had yet to be woven around it in the spirals.

Chase gasped with recognition. That had to have been Unduire! But was she real, or had that been a dream? He had no way of knowing. He tried to force himself to believe that it couldn't possibly have been real, that Unduire had been trapped in her own world until she created her talisman that she put on the Minotaur, but he couldn't be sure.

What had she been doing, leaning over his bed, watching him as he slept? Was she already implementing her evil plans, so long ago? What should he do?

This was not the time for a long, drawn-out deliberation. Silly was in danger, serious danger; now was the time for action. Chase reached down to the talisman, and closed his fist around it without looking at it. He had made his decision.

"Unduire! I hold the key to your plans in my hand! Come and fight me for it if you must have it!" he called, hoping that somehow, she was watching. That somehow, she would come.

The clearing brightened again, and Chase watched as this time, a womanly form began to take shape in front of his eyes. As she fully appeared in the clearing, Chase saw how beautiful she was, with her long, flowing hair, and her gracefully held limbs. He looked up to her face, and was hypnotized by her bright, flashing eyes.

"So you have called me at last, my son. Oh, but you didn't know that, did you? Yes, I am your mother, who abandoned you as a child, to be raised with mortal parents. I knew that you would one day attempt to destroy me, along with everything I have worked so hard to bring about. That is why I made this plan, so that you would be forced to confront me before you are truly ready. Before you can dream of defeating me," said Unduire.

Chase didn't know where to begin. Her speech, though brief, rang in his heart with a truth that he'd never encountered before. It was all true, now. It was his entire life that had been the lie. But he still had one secret weapon that the sorceress could not conquer, no matter how hard she might try. He still had Silly.

"Mother? Yes, I can see that you're telling the truth. At least, your version of the truth. You may be my mother, but I am ready to confront you. I am ready to defeat you. I am ready," said Chase.

Unduire smiled back at Chase, humoring him in his defiance.

"I know that's what you think, my son, but you've been wrong before, haven't you? You've been wrong as recently as today. And you have made your final mistake," promised Unduire.

She spread her arms wide, over her head, threw her head back, and closed her eyes. Although she didn't make a sound, Chase felt a breeze pick up around him, as all the air in the woods seemed to gather tightly around Unduire. The swirling, strengthening air currents rose above her outstretched arms, spiraling up to the sky. A torrent of leave was swept up with it, and Chase watched them tumble higher and higher. As they reached the low-lying clouds, lightning sparked in the sky, and a low rumble of thunder rolled across the ground. A sprinkle of rain began pouring down from the sky, and Chase worried about Silly's escape being hindered by the weather.

Unduire lifted her head forward again to look Chase in the eyes. At that instant, he raised the fist holding her talisman, and threw it with all his might high into the air. The great bolt of lightning that was arcing down to kill him struck the red stone instead, and shattered like glass, shards of electricity spreading far and wide, raining down on the woods from the center that was defined by the talisman.

Unduire screamed in agony. She had put so much of herself into the magic of the stone, that when it was hurt, she was injured as well. When the necklace hit the ground again, Chase took off his shirt and wrapped it around the necklace, knowing it would be burning hot. He tucked the bundle under his arms and ran from the clearing, leaving Unduire gasping for breath on the ground.

Chase only ran for a few seconds before he stopped short, unsure if he'd come out of the clearing at the same spot from which he'd entered. He didn't want to be lost and wander aimlessly, practically a sitting duck for either Unduire or the Minotaur. He looked right and left, and remained unsure which direction he should take.

Twenty-Five

Silly stumbled against a tree, trying to steady herself enough to run with everything she had, but she couldn't do anymore. Her breath came in raspy tatters through her mouth, and she could barely lift her head up enough to see where she was pointed anymore. That last run through the muddy forest was taking its toll on her energy reserves, but as she heard a whistle, fear-induced adrenaline caused her head to snap back up and her eyes to widen to their limits. It was too dark for her to make out anything that wasn't right in her face, but that didn't stop her from straining to see, holding her breath as tightly as she could, focusing all that she had into her eyes.

Nothing.

She tried to listen, with the same result. Nothing. Nothing but the rain pattering on the topmost leaves of the trees. Why couldn't it just stop raining? Why did it have to start in the first place? Why couldn't she have just stayed home, writing in her diary, being a silly little girl without a care in the world? Why couldn't he have chosen someone else, anyone else, anyone at all?

She wanted to scream, but she was too afraid that any extra sound would only lead him to her faster. Her entire plan had been erased by fear. She no longer remembered exactly what she was running from, or why she was trying to get away. She didn't know what she would do when she couldn't run any farther.

As the panic rose and rose in her mind, wreaking havoc throughout her body, he waited, patiently. He waited. He knew that she would return. He knew that she couldn't get away. He knew that she would be his, to do with as he pleased, at his pleasure.

He waited, and began to smile.

Twenty-Six

Back at home, Rachel had woken up. She'd fallen asleep immediately after dinner, and so had no idea how early it was when she woke up. Her clock on the bedside table was flashing twelve o'clock, blinking over and over. She must have snagged the cord a bit with her foot again. She always meant to tape it down, but never got around to doing it.

She walked out into the living room to check the clock on the wall. It was four in the morning. Rachel wondered if there was any chance of her going back to sleep for a few hours until it was time to wake up, but decided that probably wasn't going to happen. She sighed, shrugged her shoulders in resignation, and decided to check on Silly since she was awake anyway. She was surprised the Silly wasn't making any noise in her sleep. This was about the time that Rachel used to try to comfort her daughter.

When Rachel opened Silly's door, she expected to see her daughter's hair spread across her pillow and the covers pulled up to her neck. Rachel did not find what she expected.

The room was torn apart, as though someone had broken in and been searching for something, something small, probably, because every single item in the room was out of place. The dresser drawers were all pulled out and thrown on the floor, every book from the bookcase was strewn across the room, there were clothes lying everywhere, and the bed was in pieces.

Worst of all, Silly was nowhere to be seen.

Rachel was speechless. She didn't know what had happened. She looked to the window to see if it was broken, or at least open, but it was still securely fastened, the blinds and curtain undisturbed. Rachel took one last look around and ran across the hall to throw open Justin's door.

Justin was peacefully sleeping, sprawled across his bed as he usually was in his sleep. Nothing was more out of place than usual, which would have been hard to notice for anyone besides Rachel, as Justin was not the neatest boy when left to his own devices.

Rachel was so relieved to find her son safe and sound that she ran to his bed and snatched him up in a tight embrace, weeping. Justin was groggy and confused to be wakened in such a manner, but when Rachel let go, he sat up and rubbed his eyes.

"What's going on, Mom? Are you okay?" he asked.

"It's Silly, Silly's gone, Silly's gone!" Rachel sobbed.

Justin, much more alert now, got out of bed and went across the hall to Silly's room. He looked through the door that Rachel had left open, and was amazed by the mess. He did, however, realize that his mom was telling the truth. Silly was gone. He returned to his own room, where Rachel had collapsed on the bed, crying even harder.

"Mom? What are we going to do? Do we call the cops, or what? Should we call Chase? Do you think he knows anything about this?" Justin asked.

Rachel couldn't even hear Justin talking to her. She felt so broken in her grief. She felt that this was all her fault, that if she'd done something sooner, anything, she didn't know what, then Silly would be safe in her own bed, and none of this would have happened. She wept and wept, and Justin put his arm around her to try to offer some small comfort.

"I'll take care of it, Mom, I'll find her. It'll be okay, I promise," Justin tried to reassure her, but he wasn't sure how well it was working, and he wasn't sure that he could keep that promise.

Twenty-Seven

Rachel looked at the clock again, and wondered where in the world Silly could be. On the rare occasion that Silly was going to be late, she always, always called her mother to let her know. Silly understood how badly Rachel had been scarred by her husband's death, and would never, ever add to the fear that was always there, the fear that it had happened again. Rachel picked up the phone.

"Julia, is Silly with you? She's not? When was the last time you saw her? Do you know anyone else who might know where she is? You know it's not like her to be late and not call me. Thanks."

Rachel hung up, more and more fear coursing like lava through her veins. Julia didn't have any answers. Julia didn't have anything new to add. Where was Silly?

Rachel looked at her son, fearing he was all she had left in the world. "Justin, would you mind finishing up your homework and coming to sit at the table with me? I'd like to talk to you about Silly."

Justin packed up his books and hopped in his chair, at his mother's left hand. He knew she was worried. He was worried too. Where was his sister? Where was Silly?

Twenty-Eight

Silly had made it another quarter of a mile, most of it on her hands and knees after she kept falling to the ground, over and over. She thought as long as she could keep moving, she'd somehow be safe. It would be over if she stopped, but Silly still had fight left in her to keep moving, keep moving. She chanted to herself, aloud, in her head, she didn't know anymore. Keep moving, keep moving. Until the moment when she opened her eyes to see the leaves swaying about her head, but the branches had stopped passing her. She had stopped moving.

She heard footsteps. His footsteps. Her heart stopped beating in her chest.

Silly hadn't realized that she'd traveled in a circle. Once she was running on fear alone, she had stopped using her head completely. This had taken her back to the one place that she didn't want to be.

But as soon as she looked up and saw the Minotaur, her purpose came flooding back. She knew what she had to do. She had to fight him.

To the death.

Silly knew she couldn't outmatch this horrible beast in a battle of strength; she had to outwit him. How smart could he be, with the head of a bull? Surely if she enraged him, she could make him chase her until he was exhausted.

Then she realized that she herself was almost completely exhausted. She couldn't run around the forest for the rest of the night, and who knows how long it would take to tire the Minotaur when he only had eating Silly on his mind?

Silly's mind worked furiously. She just might have a chance. She hoped her plan would work.

She stood her ground and faced the Minotaur. He opened his furious mouth and roared his rage at her until the trees shook and branches began to cascade toward the ground. Thick, ropy saliva dripped from his slavering jaws. Silly took it all in, and waited for him to finish.

When he closed his mouth again, the Minotaur seemed to be momentarily taken aback that his prey was still waiting patiently for her demise. He didn't waste much time on that thought; instead he took one step toward her, then another.

Silly waited until the Minotaur was only a few feet away from her, then she screamed her defiance and turned around to run again.

This time, however, the monster was too enraged to wait for her to circle back around to him. He made chase, pounding the ground with feet as heavy and loud as hooves.

Silly tore through the woods again, running as thought the devil was after her. This time, however, he was. She continued on, dodging limbs with a new vigor as she led the beast into her trap.

The Minotaur came closer and closer behind Silly, the scent of her blood driving him into a more and more frenzied state. He could almost taste her. He planned to tear huge chunks of her flesh out, and then savor the rest at his leisure. Feasting was the only pleasure left to this monster, and he enjoyed it very much.

Silly risked a look over her shoulder to make sure that the Minotaur was the appropriate distance behind her. He was right where she wanted him. They were almost there. She slowed a tiny bit, allowing him to draw even closer than he had been. He reached out with his terrible clawed hands to snatch at her, and she jumped ahead of him!

Allowing the Minotaur to neatly fall into the abandoned well in which Silly had been imprisoned only a short while before.

Silly caught herself against the nearest tree, panting, out of breath. She let her trembling legs collapse beneath her to bring her to a seated position beneath the tree. She leaned her head back against its trunk, hearing nothing over the rushing of her own blood in her ears. Slowly, her breathing dropped to a more normal pace, and she lifted her head to view the pit.

The Minotaur had dropped without a sound, and Silly hadn't heard him hit the bottom, since she was breathing so heavily. She hoped against hope that the fall had killed him.

Silly waited, not wanting to risk leaning over the edge of the well if the monster had caught himself and was hanging just beneath the surface. She waited, and listened for any sounds that might come from the hole. Nothing.

Was it worth the risk to check and verify his demise? Silly was torn between her choices. Finally, caution was thrown to the wind as Silly's concern for Chase's wellbeing won out. She stretched out on the ground, and inched her way toward the well. As she neared the lip, she paused once more to listen, but still, nothing. No sound escaped the dark hole.

Finally, she screwed up her courage and peeked over the edge. Dawn was breaking, but the sun wasn't nearly high enough to cast any light down into this well. Whatever Silly had hoped she might be able to see, she was disappointed. She could only see a few feet down, and the rest faded into blackness.

Silly rolled over onto her back feeling completely defeated. She didn't know if the monster was down there, or if Unduire had spirited him away, to attack her again somewhere else. Either way, there was nothing she could do about it right now. She decided to go find Chase.

Silly stood up, brushed herself off, and trotted back toward the center of the woods. She hoped Chase hadn't done anything stupid, and was still waiting for her there.

Twenty-Nine

Chase had done something stupid.

Chase was lost.

The only good thing about being lost, he thought, was that Unduire wouldn't know where he was, either.

He had tried to do as Silly had, to follow a straight line of trees to get to one side of the woods, but he knew he had to be doing something wrong. He'd been walking for hours, and the sun was starting to come up. He wondered if he'd be able to find his way back to the clearing; surely Silly would look for him there first.

Chase stopped to laugh at himself. The whole reason he was here was to rescue Silly, and here he was waited to be rescued by her. Sometimes things turn out nothing at all like you'd expect. At least it was the middle of summer, and he wasn't freezing to death by walking around with his shirt wrapped around some magical item that could either save the world or destroy it. He sighed.

These trees seemed a bit familiar, and Chase wondered if he was walking in circles. He'd heard that people tend to do that. He just hoped he was circling in the right direction.

Suddenly, he realized that he could hear footsteps that weren't his own. They weren't thundering through the woods, so he was relieved that it wasn't the Minotaur, but was it Silly, or his mother? He crouched behind a tree to wait and see.

Silly tapped Chase on the shoulder and laughed when he nearly jumped out of his skin.

"You're no woodsman, that's for sure!" she said, still laughing.

"Silly! Is he still chasing you? Are you okay?" asked Chase, worried.

"I'm okay, now. I don't know if he's dead or if Unduire whisked him away at the last minute, but either way, he's not bothering us right this minute. Why didn't you stay in the clearing? You would have been safe there. I had a plan, and it worked," said Silly.

"I wasn't safe. Unduire showed up. I hope I kept her busy enough that you took care of the Minotaur for good. What was your plan, and how did it work?" asked Chase.

"I tricked him into following me back to the old well that I was trapped in a few hours ago," said Silly. "I dodged at just the right instant and he kept going and fell right in. I tried to look over the side to make sure he was dead, but it was too dark for me to see the bottom. I didn't hear any sounds coming up from the bottom, though, so I'm pretty sure that it worked. Now tell me about Unduire, what did she say to you?"

Chase took a deep breath, trying to organize his tumbling thoughts before he answered Silly. He couldn't believe that such a simple plan had outwitted the Minotaur! Still, the monster wasn't supposed to be highly intelligent. Even so, it was a completely crazy plan, but it had worked, so Chase was very glad indeed that Silly was safe.

"Silly, I'm just going to come out and say this so I can know what your reaction is without having to waste time worrying. Unduire is my mother," confessed Chase.

"Your mother? But how? How can she be your mother? And if she is, then—that's how she's known what you're doing all along, isn't it? She's been keeping tabs on you your whole life, and she's just been using you for her own sick, twisted agenda. That's horrible!" said Silly.

Thirty

Back at Silly's apartment, Rachel had calmed down somewhat, and was frantically trying to find someone who could help her and Justin find her daughter.

Justin was in Silly's room, digging through the mess, trying to find some clue that would help them have some idea of where to start looking. Rachel had called and called Chase, but had never gotten an answer. Julia hadn't had any idea, and Justin didn't dare suggest to his mother his greatest fear: that Silly had gone into the woods to fight the monster.

When he finished sorting the mess into piles, Justin realized the one thing that was missing, along with Silly. Her running shoes. He knew it was time to break the news to his mother.

Rachel was on the phone with the police. She screamed, "What do you mean you can't do anything? She's a child, she's missing, and you have to do *something*!"

The dispatcher tried again, unsuccessfully, to calm Rachel down. "I'm sending an officer to you right now; he'll take all your information, and a recent picture of your daughter will help greatly. I'm sorry you're going through this. We will do what we can to help you."

Rachel dropped the phone and sank to the floor next to it. Her head dropped to her hands, and she cried great, wracking sobs that shook her whole body. All she could think of was Dennis. Dennis hadn't come home that night; he never came home again. She couldn't go through that again with her daughter.

Justin tried to comfort his mother as best he could, but she wouldn't respond to his arm around her shoulders. He had always thought of himself as the man of the house, since he'd never even met his father, but at ten years old, he finally knew that those shoes were just too big for him to fill yet.

But he had to tell Rachel what he'd learned from Silly's room.

"Mom? You have to listen to me. I know where Silly is," Justin tried to get through to her.

Rachel continued to cry, but she did seem to be trying to stop enough to listen to what Justin had to say.

"Mom, Silly's in the woods. I know that's where she's gone. She's gone to fight the monster that's in the woods. I don't think there's anything we can do right now but wait. I'll tell you what I know, but you have to believe me. Can you promise to believe what I'm telling you, no matter how crazy it sounds?" Justin asked, tears in his eyes.

Rachel quieted herself enough to speak a few words.

"I can try. Please tell me."

"After dinner, when you fell asleep in your room, I snuck back down the hall to listen to Silly talk to Chase. Silly is like some kind of secret weapon that Chase and some other people like him have been searching for. She's the only one who can beat the monster that's trying to come into our world and destroy it," began Justin.

Rachel stared in disbelief.

"Are you saying that those dreams she's been having actually mean something? I knew there was more to them that she would share with me!" cried Rachel.

"That's it, Mom. There was this witch a long time ago that put a spell on the Minotaur that was still alive in her world. She locked it away between worlds somewhere, but it got out, and now it's trying to break through to our world, here. Silly has to put some necklace on it to banish it again. I don't know how she's supposed to do that, because she doesn't know where the necklace went, but I'm pretty sure that's she's either trying to find it now, or she already has it, and that's why she went to the woods, to put it back on that monster. She's a hero, Mom, and we have to let her be a hero, or nothing will ever be the same again," finished Justin.

"I can't let her do that!" screamed Rachel. "I can't let her go try to be some kind of magical hero that she's not! She's just a girl, she's my daughter!" Rachel collapsed back to the floor, but she'd already cried every tear she had. Her limp body cried out her despair.

"Mom, you have to get up. You already called the police, so they're going to be on their way. They could be here any minute. You have to be able to help them fill out their paperwork so they can look for Silly, but don't tell them about this. Please don't tell them," Justin begged his mother.

Rachel's voice was muffled by her arm draped over her face. "I know I can't tell them that, Justin. They'll laugh at me and think I'm crazy, and they might take you away with them. They might even arrest me for something, I don't know. But you're right. I have to talk to them when they get here. You're not suggesting that—that you go to the woods to look for Silly, are you? Please don't do that, Justin, I need you here, now more than ever," Rachel asked.

"I don't know what I'm suggesting, Mom. I want to help find her, but I don't want to get in her way. I don't want her to see me out there and be distracted when she should be paying attention to something else. I don't want me looking for her to be the reason she gets hurt," he said.

The two of them looked up as they heard a knock on the front door. That had to be the police.

"Okay, Justin, just go to your room and wait while I talk to them. I'll come get you when they're gone, so please, just wait," Rachel asked.

Justin agreed, and headed down the hall and into his room, where he closed the door behind him.

Rachel stood up, shakily, and went to answer the front door. She didn't check to peephole before unlocking the deadbolt and turning the knob, so she was surprised to see standing there, instead of a uniformed officer, a beautiful woman with long red hair and a slight smile on her face.

"Hello, Rachel. I hear there's a bit of a problem with your daughter," said Unduire, stepping through the open door and strolling into the living room to have a seat on the most comfortable chair in the room.

"Who are you?" asked Rachel, confused. "You're not with the police department, are you?"

"Ugh!" Unduire made a face of disgust at the mention. "I got rid of those idiots on my way to your door. They tried to tell me I was acting suspiciously, whatever that means. They won't be bothering you tonight; I can assure you of that."

Rachel turned her head and seemed to become aware that she was still standing there, holding the door open for no one. She closed it and joined her visitor in the living room.

"Really, who are you, then? And how did you know my name? You're not a renter, I'm sure of that," said Rachel.

Unduire laughed aloud at the thought that she, a sorceress, would ever live somewhere like this, packed among the idiot mortals like sardines in a can.

"I am your dream come true, my dear," Unduire told Rachel. "I can help you find your daughter, and all you have to do is help me just one tiny bit."

"You know where Silly is? Oh, I'll do anything to have her back here, safe and sound again. Please, tell me, what do you need?" Rachel asked.

"It's a mere trifle, really. Something I could do for myself if I just had the time to spare. I need you to return my necklace to me. Your daughter has stolen it from its rightful owner, I would never try to cast aspersions on another woman's parenting, but the truth is the truth, and your daughter is a thief."

"I don't know what you're talking about, but if it gets my Silly back home, I don't care what you call her. What does this necklace look like?" asked Rachel.

""It's something that's been in my family for a long time. A very long time. Though the setting has had to be changed, the dark red stone in the center has remained with us forever."

As Unduire continued her description, Rachel was horrified to realize that she must be speaking of the necklace that has affected Silly so deeply when Julia had found it on the night of her birthday. Rachel didn't need anyone to tell her that this woman was up to no good, even if she was promising to return Silly home. Rachel wasn't sure what she could do to get this woman out of her home without the necklace, which she knew wasn't anywhere in the apartment. Rachel began to fear that she would have to find the necklace in order to find Silly, and she didn't know how she would be able to do that.

"You look a little disturbed, dear, haven't you been paying attention? How in this world will you know my necklace when you find it if you haven't been listening?" asked Unduire, in her beautiful voice, dripping with false sincerity.

"No, I was just trying to think if I'd ever seen anything like that before," Rachel stuttered. "I don't believe your necklace has ever been in my apartment. Don't you think it would be easier to ask Silly about it when she comes back home?"

"She's not coming home without my property. And I know it's nowhere in your filthy dwelling. Your daughter has given it to someone else, a boy. And he, I might add, is no good for her. She'll be quite disappointed to find out who he really is," Unduire smiled again, a little more wickedly this time.

Rachel was terrified to hear that this person knew so much about what was going on when Rachel felt like she barely even knew what was real anymore. She only hoped that Justin stayed in his room, and that he wouldn't get hurt.

"We'll just sit here and wait. She will come to me," promised Unduire. "She will come to me, or she will die trying, and that is all the same to me."

"What danger is she in out there? Please, if you know, just tell me," begged Rachel.

Unduire laughed a silky smooth laugh.

"We shall see."

Thirty-One

Silly was not exactly disappointed. She was devastated for her new friend Chase, the good person she could not reconcile with the evil impression that Unduire had made on her each time they'd met. Silly had always believed that parents were a reflection of their children, or the other way around, she could never make up her mind which. Either way, they were made from the same mold.

But Chase was nothing like his mother. If she even was his mother.

"Chase! How do you know she's telling the truth? Maybe she meant something else and you just took it as she was saying that she's your mom," suggested Silly.

"It's true, Silly. I remember. I remember her leaning over me in my cradle, singing to me. And the necklace she wore, it had the same stone as this one. It had this very stone in it," Chase said as he held up his shirt, still bundled around the talisman so he wouldn't risk its touch on his bare skin.

"You have the necklace? How—you have to tell me what happened after I led the Minotaur away from you. I'm completely lost. Okay, what happened?" asked Silly.

Chase related the story to Silly as they began walking, heading back toward the clearing.

"When you two were gone, I saw something in the clearing, and it turned out to be the talisman. I was able to drop it just before I was captured by its spell, but then Unduire appeared, just like the Minotaur did. She told me she was my mother, and I remembered. But then she tried to kill me. She used her magic to bring up this storm, and I threw the necklace into a bolt of lightning. That really hurt her. I think this thing that I have is actually a part of her, somehow. I picked it back up and wrapped it so I couldn't touch it or see it, and I ran. And then you finally found me," Chase finished, still ashamed that he'd run off only to get lost himself.

Silly's mind was boggled.

"That story puts mine to shame, Chase, and I killed a Minotaur! But that does sound like good news to me; if Unduire was attacking you with that gigantic bolt of lightning I saw, that means she couldn't have had time to save her pet, and he's really defeated. At least we don't have to worry about him anymore, right?" she asked.

"That's a good point, Silly. I hope I hurt her a lot more than it looked like. I hope she's still hurt in the center of the—clearing," Chase broke off as the two of them reentered the same clearing in which their real adventure had begun.

It was completely empty, except for the damp dead leaves on the ground.

"Where could she have gone? She found you; do you think she's after me? That would lead her back—I have to go home right now!" cried Silly, panicking.

Chase grabbed her arm before she could begin running back to her apartment.

"If she's already there, it may be too late for your family. Do you have any idea how mad she's going to be about the Minotaur? She was already mad enough to try to kill me, and I'm her own son, even though that doesn't mean very much to her. She'll still care less about your family. You're right, we need to go back, but we need to be even more careful than we have been, especially because we really haven't been careful at all tonight," explained Chase.

"But what can we do to get rid of her? I know she's not going to fall for any stupid 'make her fall down a well' plan," said Silly.

"You're right about that, but there has to be something we can do. We just have to figure it out before she does anything to us or your family. I really don't think that she'll do anything until we show up. She probably wants you to see exactly what she's capable of. But all bets are off once we walk in that door. We have to work everything out before we leave the woods," Chase said.

Silly sat down in the middle of the clearing, near tears and ready to give up.

"I don't know what I was thinking. I have to be asleep. I have to be asleep! I have to be dreaming this whole thing. Who goes out and kills monsters in their back yard? Who hangs out with thousand year old boys who are sons of evil sorceresses from another dimension? This is absolutely nuts. There must be something seriously wrong with me."

She put her hands up to cover her face and slowly leaned back until she was lying on the ground. A sound that was half sob and half laugh escaped her mouth. She dropped her hands down to rest her sides and felt the dead leaves on the ground to either side of her body. She relaxed her legs and let them drop until her knees were flat on the ground. Finally, Silly closed her eyes and wished with all her heart that she would wake up, safe and sound in her own bed, and that all of this, the past few weeks, the monsters, the bad dreams, and the necklace, had been made up by her sleeping mind.

Silly opened her eyes.

She lay on her back, fully relaxed, in a clearing in the woods, with Chase standing over her. Nothing had changed. At that moment, she knew that this was real. They had to come up with some kind of plan to save Rachel and Justin, and they had to do it right now.

Silly turned her head to look at Chase. He looked so tired, exhausted, and he was filthy from that bit of rain that had turned the ground to mud. He was still shirtless. He looked at her with such desperation that she couldn't let him down. Just like she couldn't let her family down. Just like she couldn't let the whole world down.

No one but Chase even knew that they were counting on Silly, but Silly knew. Silly felt the weight of that burden pushing her against the ground more firmly than gravity ever could. She closed her eyes again, but pushed her hands against the ground to lift her body to a sitting position. She crossed her legs.

Silly opened her eyes to beckon Chase to sit on the ground in front of her. He looked a little confused, but decided to sit anyway. He crossed his legs and gracefully sank down to the forest floor. Silly held out both of her hands to Chase, and he reached out to take them firmly in his own.

"I know what we have to do," said Silly.

"Tell me," Chase simply replied.

Silly closed her eyes, took a deep breath through her nostrils, and opened her eyes to stare deeply into Chase's.

"This necklace that she made," Silly gestured at the bundled shirt lying on the ground next to Chase, "This thing has the power to do the same to her that it did to the Minotaur. She didn't cast enough of her spells to prevent someone using it against her. She never suspected that anyone would ever know enough about her magic to understand what she did. She truly believes that she's better enough than everyone else who ever lived, and that gives her the right to rule every world that ever was, is or will be. She's not. But we are.

"We have to go make sure that she's at my apartment. If she's not there, we have to find her, wherever she is. We have to find her, and we have to catch her with her own evil magic.

"I know she tried to kill you, and I know that she was able to use her magic to that end. But she can't kill me. If she was able to, she would have done it earlier tonight instead of just trying to stick me at the bottom of a well where I couldn't get out by myself. She hadn't counted on you being here to help me. She makes mistakes, Chase, and we have to exploit them.

"She thinks we're idiots. We have to make sure she continues to think that. We have to burst into my apartment, guns blazing, well, figuratively speaking. I'm sorry, Chase, but you're going to have to distract her. I know you thought that I was the one risking my life, but I'm afraid that you're going to be the one risking his life. There's a chance we're not both going to make it through the night.

"But you knew that, didn't you? You're here because there's a chance that no one is going to make it through this night. We're going to make sure that this world survives, Chase. This world, and all of the others are going to live on and on, with or without us.

"Can you do this? Are you with me?" Silly asked, all seriousness now that they were down to the wire.

Chase had been holding Silly's hands throughout her speech, keeping eye contact even when he wanted to run. He only had one word left to say.

"Yes."

They rose as one, and Silly bent to pick up Chase's shirt with its precious cargo. As she began to shake the shirt out to drop the talisman, Chase reached to stop her.

"Silly, don't. I need you here, and you know what happens when you touch that thing."

"It won't happen anymore. I know the trick to it now," Silly answered.

She gave the shirt a sharp snap downward, and the necklace fell to the ground. Silly handed Chase's shirt back to him, and bent to pick up the necklace by the pendant. Chase opened his mouth to protest, but he was too late. Silly was already touching it. She closed her fist around it, and squeezed tightly. When she opened her hand again, the chain had fallen away, and the talisman was left alone, unfettered, in her palm.

Silly rolled the red stone and its surrounding wires gently in her fingers. When she had the talisman turned exactly how she wanted it, she squeezed her fist closed again.

This time when she opened her hand, there was a change in the very stone itself. Chase was amazed to see that the stone wasn't the deep, dark, sinister, uniform red that it had always been before. There was now a bright flaw in the very center of the stone, and a blazing light seeped forth from the crack. Silly closed her hand once more around it, but the light still found its way out of her hand between her fingers.

Chase was speechless at what he had just seen. He didn't know how Silly knew what she knew, or how she did what she did, but he tried to take it in stride, and matched her pace as she left the clearing, heading out of the woods for good.

As they walked, Silly led the way, and Chase tried to work up the courage to walk along by her side, but all he could do was follow, bewildered at the turn his seemingly simple mission had taken.

It was full daylight now, and the light was streaming through the trees. Chase continued to follow Silly, not seeing anything besides her. She seemed to glow brighter with every step she took.

Finally, they came to the edge of the tree line, and Silly continued to lead the way across the parking lot and down the corridor leading to her apartment.

She only slowed to a stop as they reached her front door. Chase noticed that Silly seemed much taller now, because she carried herself differently, with more confidence. He wondered if she would knock or walk in. It was her apartment after all, but if Unduire was inside, Chase would welcome any seconds between now and meeting her again that he could get.

Silly put her hand on the doorknob and turned it. As she pushed the door open, Chase saw a strange smile on her face, and he was afraid. It wasn't fear for Silly's safety, or for his own; Chase feared for life itself, in every shape and form it had ever taken.

Unduire was there, sitting calmly with Rachel in the living room. Chase hadn't even fully entered the apartment before they both stood up, and Rachel opened her mouth to scream. Chase saw that Unduire wore the same strange smile as Silly, and suddenly, he realized what was wrong.

He was wrong. Everything was wrong. Their whole plan was wrong. If he didn't do something right now, Unduire would win. As a flood of adrenaline dumped into Chase's bloodstream, he saw Justin leap out from the hallway to knock Rachel to the floor and protect her with his own body.

Chase saw his opportunity, and gripped the shirt that he'd never bothered to put back on, but continued to carry during their trek back to the apartment from the clearing. He took one giant step and holding the hem in one hand and the collar in the other, threw his makeshift rope around Silly's neck and pulled with all his might.

Just as Unduire lifted one perfectly manicured, wickedly clawed hand to strike Silly down, Chase yanked Silly to the floor. When she hit the ground, at first he feared that he had killed her, because her arms fell to either side of her body and her eyes softly closed. Chase could ill afford the moment of panic that gripped him. But he was quickly relieved to see her moan and slightly wince.

Unduire froze midstrike, and a fury like no one had ever seen grew in her eyes. She shifted her gaze to Chase, and curled her fingers into a fist. Raising her fist high, she chanted a few words that Chase could barely hear, let alone understand. But he knew they could only mean trouble for him.

Somehow he knew the right instant to duck, and the bolt of lightning passed directly where he'd been standing, to crash through the front window and disappear outside. Silly had hit the floor hard when she went down, and she groaned and put one hand to her head. But she wasn't glowing anymore.

Unduire was now the center of all illumination in the apartment. She spread her arms wide, and seemed to rise even taller than she already stood, towering over her four victims.

Justin and Rachel lay on the floor in the living room, clutching at each other, terrified, not having any real idea of what was going on, other than big trouble. They both closed their eyes and hugged each other, believing these would be their last seconds.

Silly lay almost still on the floor beside the couch, but she certainly wasn't completely alert yet after Chase had pulled her down. She didn't even seem to be aware of anything around her right now.

Chase was the only person able to watch what Unduire was preparing to do with any objectivity or understanding. He'd already given up any hope that he once might have had of surviving this day. Silly was the only person left who he truly cared about, and he was ready to die for her, or with her if he had to.

Sparking balls of blue fire began to grow above the palm of each of Unduire's hands as she continued her incantations. She brought her arms straight up above her head and kept going until they were crossed in front of her body. With another of her infamous smiles, Unduire said her final words:

"Goodbye for now, my son."

With that pronouncement, Unduire flashed out of this world in a burst of bright blue fire.

Chase frantically looked around on the floor surrounding Silly's outstretched hand, but the talisman that they had fought so hard to retrieve and keep was nowhere to be seen. Chase dropped his head to the ground in surrender. The stone was gone with Unduire, and the only chance they had to save themselves was gone with it.

It was all Chase's fault; if he hadn't knocked Silly to the ground, she wouldn't have lost her grip on the red stone. He couldn't believe he had failed so horribly. What was he going to do? The worst feeling of all, though, was that he had let Silly down. He didn't know how he was going to live with that knowledge for another minute.

Then Silly propped herself up on one elbow and looked at Chase.

"She's really gone," Silly marveled. "I can feel that she's gone."

"She'll be back," Chase pointed out.

"But we'll have a warning. I'll know when she's coming back, and we can be ready to beat her. If we don't, then I'll know the next time, and the next, forever. I'm connected to her now, and she can't do anything about that. I don't know what she's thinking, but I do know that she's retreated. It's going to be a long time before we have to do anything like this again, Chase."

Rachel and Justin looked at each other, confused. Again?

"Young lady, you're never disappearing in the middle of the night without letting me know, for as long as you live. Do you have any idea of what we've had to deal with in this home while you were out doing who knows what?" Rachel began to lecture.

"I'm sorry Mom, I know how worried you must have been, but you have to understand that I'm not just a kid anymore. I'm a guardian. When I'm called, I have to go protect this world and all of the others," said Silly.

Chase stared at Silly in wonder. Without him ever telling her, she knew what she needed to say. She knew what she was and she knew what her vows were. At that moment, he knew how much he loved her. His face lit up in a smile and his heart felt like it would burst from excitement.

"Silly?" he asked.

"Yes, my love?" she replied.

"Are you sure you can do this?" he asked, blushing that she would call him her love.

"I have to," was all she needed to say.

21219566R00099

Made in the USA
Lexington, KY
08 March 2013